A DECENT KILLER

A DECENT KILLER

Jeanne Hart

Chivers Press • G.K. Hall & Co.
Bath, Avon, England • Thorndike, Maine, USA

This Large Print edition is published by Chivers Press, England, and by G.K. Hall & Co., USA.

Published in 1995 in the U.K. by arrangement with HarperCollins Publishers.

Published in 1995 in the U.S. by arrangement with Vicky Bijur Literary Agency.

U.K. Hardcover   ISBN 0-7451-2900-5 (Chivers Large Print)
U.K. Softcover   ISBN 0-7451-2909-9 (Camden Large Print)
U.S. Softcover   ISBN 0-7838-1139-X (Nightingale Collection Edition)

Originally published in 1991 by HarperCollins Publishers, London.

The text of this Large Print edition is unabridged.
Other aspects of the book may vary from the original edition.

Set in 16 pt. New Times Roman.

Printed in Great Britain on acid-free paper.

British Library Cataloguing in Publication Data available

Library of Congress Cataloging-in-Publication Data

Hart, Jeanne.
    A decent killer / Jeanne Hart.
        p.   cm.
    ISBN 0-7838-1139-X (alk. paper : lg. print)
    1. Large type books.   I. Title.
[PS3558.A6816D43   1995]
813'.54—dc20   94-34003

SATURDAY

CHAPTER ONE

Max Follett took the steps two at a time and pushed open the heavy door of the post office, his big bearlike body nearly upsetting a woman who was leaving in the same haste. As he took his place in the dwindling line before the open window, he checked the wall clock. Another five minutes and Saturday hours would have been over. Now that, he thought, would have been the final irony. My moment of triumph. The manuscript finally finished, edited, typed, packaged, in hand, and I arrive to find the post office closed—the mails totally, irrevocably inaccessible for two days.

'Next.'

He stepped forward and surrendered the package to the postal clerk. She was a sad, grey-faced woman, but she brightened as she took it. 'Oh. Mr Follett. Off to the publisher's?' Everyone in town knew he had just finished a book.

He grinned. 'Certified. Valuable property.' Standing there watching her fill out the forms—she was doing it for him, probably as a result of the grin—he had an overwhelming impulse to appeal to her, to beg her to give it back. With a dragging sense of letdown, he saw the manuscript disappear into a canvas bin.

Walking down the post office steps—more leisurely now, his appointment wasn't for another fifteen minutes—he reflected wryly that he was surely the only person in Bay Cove for whom his finishing of the manuscript produced a sense of desolation. His colleagues and his students must have reacted quite differently. Much as they admired him—and liked him, he was sure they did—they most likely were damned glad to hear the last of it.

And his neighbours, some of whom had lived through that ten-year struggle with him, obviously felt such relief that they had to celebrate. No, that wasn't fair. The party that night was one of congratulation. After a long dry period, everyone would be vying to entertain him now, just as they had after that first award-winning book ten years ago, but this gathering was different. These were friends. He squared his shoulders and strode down the tree-lined outdoor mall towards the coffee house at which he was to meet his former wife, Florence.

*   *   *

They had arranged to meet in a back booth of the Saltcellar, a spot never frequented by people they knew and for the most part a high school hangout. As she greeted him, he registered with amusement that she was going

2

to keep things pleasant; that was Florence, ever optimistic.

She smiled at him over her coffee-cup, almost flirtatious. 'How's the Great Author?'

'One book greater at least. I just mailed it.'

'That's wonderful, Max. You must be so— relieved. To have it done, I mean.'

'I am. I am. A little let down, too. I'm not sure whether that's the prospect of undertaking another or just the feeling of having lost a constant companion.' He laughed. 'Well.' He picked up his coffee-cup. 'What's this all about?'

'It's really a very little thing to ask.'

'Of an old bedmate. A discarded bedmate.' The words were out before he could check them. He had never forgiven her for leaving him.

She knew and sighed. 'Max.'

'I'm sorry. I know it's all water under the bridge. I should keep my mouth shut.' He looked at her more closely. 'You're looking tired, Flossie. No trouble at home?'

'No.' She looked away.

He reached across the narrow table and took her hand. 'Arthur's not hanging around the nursery at night, crooning to the crocuses? Maybe he's working up to some Roethkian excesses about his devouring infants.' He removed his hand. 'I don't seem able to speak of him without sounding malicious, do I?'

'No, you don't. You know, Arthur never did

3

anything to you, Max.'

He raised his eyebrows.

'Well, he didn't. I met him *after* we separated, remember? And I don't know what you're talking about, anyway.'

'No, I suppose you wouldn't. You do look tired, though, a little pinched. Peaked, I guess we call it. Granted that Arthur never did anything to me, sometimes I think you've completely forgotten that we had our moments too, Flossie.' He smiled faintly. 'We should have gone ahead and let you have that baby. Maybe we'd still be together.' After a moment he added, 'Not that you seem to be having one with Arthur. Don't you know time's running out, babe? God knows you never had any problem with fecundity. It isn't that Arthur's—?' He stopped.

'I should have saved both of us the trouble of coming down here,' she said, her voice cold.

He thought: So that's it, and took her hands again, both of them, in his. He was surprised to find how sad for her he felt. 'I'll stop. I will. Now. Tell me exactly what it is I'm to do.'

She said nothing.

'Come on, Floss, tell me. I'll behave.'

She raised her eyes to him and drew her hands away. 'Well...' she began.

Listening to her, he thought: The thing that really hurts is that only Florence has really known me. Only Florence. He was aware of a yearning towards her.

4

*   *   *

On the way home, he couldn't resist dropping in at the nursery, admiring the new wing and exclaiming over an exotic plant. In passing, he let drop the remark. It seemed offhand, but he had got through, he knew he had. Strange he could feel pity for Florence and none at all for her husband.

Driving home, he thought about Arthur. Arthur and Florence. The three of them met often enough, had since the first bitterness was past. Civilized, adult, that was what they had been. But in part that was because Arthur had always refused to submit to his feelings about Max, as though they were somehow demeaning. But Max knew he had them, just as he had feelings about Arthur. He sighed. It was complicated, civilized or not.

By the time he pulled up before his house, he had sloughed off the mild depression he had felt since the mailing of the book. He was feeling warm towards the world and, when he saw Perry Devane and young Marcie Terpstra standing next door in front of Perry's house, even neighbourly.

He walked back towards them. 'The deed is done. The manuscript is in the mail.'

'You must be pleased,' said Marcie. 'Now you really do have something to celebrate.' In the sun, her head was like a copper penny.

5

He turned to Perry. 'Now if I were like you—a book a year.'

Her eyes were suspicious. 'You know that's entirely different, Max.' She extended a hand. 'Congratulations.'

'It may be different, but I envy you, really I do.' He looked away. 'It's so damned *hard* for me.'

'My books don't receive the attention yours do.'

'That may be. I'd give a good deal to be more prolific and have less attention paid.' He stopped for a minute longer. 'You're looking good, Perry. You've done something to your hair.'

She looked pleased. 'Just a different haircut. I'm surprised you noticed.'

'I notice,' he said, his eyes intent on her. She stepped back. He could see she was wondering if he was flirting with her, thinking he knew better.

'Max,' Marcie said, 'Leona's waiting for you.'

His eyes moved towards his house. 'Ah, Leona.' He turned away and then took a step back. 'May I walk you up the hill tonight, Marcie? I need moral support if I'm to be celebrated.' Remembering, he added, 'And you, Perry?'

Marcie said, 'We're going up with the Blochs. Why don't you just join us? Otherwise, we'll see you up there.' She turned back to

Perry, dismissal clear in the lines of her back, the tilt of her head.

'Another time,' he said. He cast a last glance at Marcie and started towards his own house.

*　　　*　　　*

She had her own key and was waiting in the living-room, lying back in the big chair, the one he always sat in, her long bare legs stretched before her, her sandals off, her smooth dark head resting against the back. He never got used to her, the purity of that face above the ripe invitation that was her body. A study in contradictions. He could not escape it: she was different from anything—anyone—he had ever known. He had met no one to match her. It must have been like that with men and Marilyn Monroe, the incredible impish child-face, the rich body, the sense of having achieved the unachievable. Ah, Leona, he thought, it's a shame...

He dropped into the chair opposite her. 'Here to congratulate me? I just put it in the mail. My patient editor will be exulting.'

'No, I didn't come down for that, but congratulations, anyway. I came to let you know something.'

'Yes?' He felt a tug of anxiety.

'Max, I've always said we'd celebrate when the book was finally done. I want tonight to be nice, a good party, so I want to say this before

7

we all get together, not to cast any shadows on the evening. I did mean what I said the other night, Max. We really are finished. As lovers, I mean. We've meant something to each other and I don't want us to part with hard feelings, but I think you know as well as I do that it's pretty much over, all but the goodbyes.'

He looked at her.

She returned his glance sadly. 'Somehow, I have the feeling that none of this is news to you.'

The surge of feeling surprised him and the sense of loss. Keep things in perspective, Max, he sharply reminded himself.

To her he said, with truth, 'Not news. But maybe harder to accept than you think.'

She said nothing.

'Let's keep what's good, Leona? Friends?'

'Yes, friends.' She laughed. 'Maybe that'll be easier.' She leaned forward to slip her sandals on. When she sat up her face was suffused with rose.

'God, you're beautiful,' he said. He could have bitten his tongue.

'Thank you.' She stood up, something ironic in her smile. 'I know you do appreciate beauty.' She put out her hand. 'I would like to return this.'

'The formal final act?' But he took it from her.

'Goodbye, Max. I'll see you at the party tonight.' She bent and kissed his cheek. 'Don't

8

get up.' She walked from the room.

He sat stroking the key. The heaviness that had overtaken him in the post office descended again. Even thoughts of his plans for the future would not dispel his sense of stinging defeat. If he had let himself, he would have wept.

MONDAY

CHAPTER TWO

Detective-Sergeant Carl Pedersen backed the car out of the parking space, his face grim. This was a call he was not eager to take and his partner, Ronald Tate, was making things no easier.

'Follett?' Tate said, his tone accusing. 'Not *Max* Follett?'

'Max Follett, the writer. Our resident celebrity.'

'He's dead? You're *sure*? He's so young.'

Pedersen nodded. 'I'm afraid so.' He shook his head. 'He was about forty-eight, I think. Crazy circumstances. A hair-drier.'

'What?' The usually mild-mannered Tate scowled as though the senior detective were making a bad joke. 'That's absurd.'

'Beneath his dignity? The story is that he was in the tub, one of the enclosed kind, showering. He'd been electrocuted. The drier had fallen in the tub.'

9

'Follett used a hair-drier?' Tate sounded shocked. Then he said, his tone still aggrieved, 'He's just finished his second book—finally. Like Styron's second; I hear that was quite a wait, too. It was coming out in the fall.' Tate was the son of a librarian, a fact he claimed accounted for his passion for order as well as for his love of books. 'Who found him?' he said.

'The woman next door.' Pedersen turned into the boulevard that led steeply to the campus area. 'She said she knew his routine and something seemed wrong.'

'Sounds fishy. Who is she? Someone from the university?'

'No, a writer, too. Her name is Perry Devane.'

'Devane. That's that Gothic writer. Romances? There was a big spread on her in the *Banner* a couple weeks ago. She writes bestsellers.'

Pedersen looked blank. After a moment he said, 'You know what you remind me of? Me and Camus. Freda was a lit. major when we were in college and she brought books along every time we had a date.' He smiled. 'She was broadening me. I remember we talked for hours about *The Stranger*. That was when I still had the illusion that I'd work in civil service for a while and then go back to school and study criminology or psychology. Something.' He swung the car left into a main

10

road, climbed the hill and turned right into a side-street.

'You like what you do,' Tate said as Pedersen braked.

'I'm not complaining. You just remind me of how I felt when I heard Camus was killed in that car crash. I kept thinking, "No, it's got to be a mistake. Camus can't be *dead*."' He grinned. 'It probably hit me harder because I didn't know that many French novelists.'

Tate nodded. 'It is a shock. Follett was no Camus, but that first book was damned good.'

The side-street on which they had parked was in need of paving. Set back from street was a pair of houses, one of weathered shingle, rambling, and squat enough to be partially concealed by overgrown eugenia bushes. On its left, a matter of fifteen feet away, a second house, apparently a product of the same builder, had been given a certain elegance with putty-grey paint and black trim, but it echoed the plan of the unpainted building. Each house was flanked on its far side by an open field. In one, two horses calmly grazed in the bright sunlight.

Pedersen and Tate approached the grey-painted building. The woman who met them at the door had clipped white hair that stood on end as though she had run her fingers through it many times. The erect bearing and patrician good looks did not accord with her distraught appearance, nor did the overlay of tan conceal

11

her pallor.

'Mrs Devane. Detective Pedersen. This is Detective Tate. It was you who phoned the police?'

'Miss. It's Miss Devane. Yes. I—found him.' She turned her head towards the house next door. 'That officer says he's dead. I thought so, I was afraid to check and see. The shower was still running.'

Pedersen raised his eyebrows. 'You were smart to be careful. Could we ask you to come next door with us so we can find out exactly what you saw?'

She nodded. 'It isn't what you think. I'm just his neighbour.'

'I don't think anything, Miss Devane. Are you all right?' He held out a hand.

She shrugged away from it. 'Fine,' she said, and pushed past to precede them to Follett's house.

Leaving her in the living-room with Patrol Officer Muller, they walked through to the bathroom. It was of the same vintage as the house, late 'fifties, unremodelled: a pair of sinks beneath a mirror along the left wall with, beyond, a walled compartment for the toilet; a tub on the far right-hand side, its sliding doors of pebbled glass. On the wall facing them, at a right-angle to the tub, was a long, narrow, high window, open half way, of frosted glass with a wide sill. The cord of the drier had been plugged into a wall socket beneath the window and led to the tub; the far shower door had been slid back just enough to accommodate the girth of the drier. The other shower door had been opened when Muller had turned off the shower.

Pedersen leaned over and peered in, touching nothing. Tate watched wordlessly. Pedersen straightened. 'Looks like an old hair-drier. I should think driers are pretty well protected against this sort of thing these days, people are so careless. Even so, it must have been some kind of freak situation.' He paused, thoughtful. 'He's down here at the faucet end, his back turned to the drier.'

'How could it have fallen in? If he kept it on the window-sill, it'd have landed on the floor. Could it have been suicide?'

Pedersen frowned. 'Suicides by electrocution aren't common. Besides, that shower door was opened just enough to slip the drier in. If he were trying to commit suicide, would he have worried about getting the bathroom floor wet?'

Tate looked at the shower doors. 'Right. That means—'

'Let's radio a dead body call and get the crime scene boys over here.'

'We're assuming foul play?'

'Let's say the circumstances merit investigation. It's not likely to be an accident.' He shrugged. 'Any ten-year-old knows electricity and water don't mix. I think

13

someone wanted Mr Follett not to see the publication of his second book.'

*   *   *

Pedersen left Tate waiting for the crime scene investigators and accompanied Perry Devane back to her house. Warm as the day was, she wrapped her arms around her body and shivered. In the kitchen, she indicated a chair. 'Coffee's still hot.' Without asking, she poured a cup for him and one for herself and sat down opposite him.

'This has been a shock for you,' Pedersen said, 'but I do have to ask you a few questions.'

She cast an oblique glance at the notebook he had taken out and sat watching him, silent.

'That's Devane—one word?'

She nodded.

'You're a writer?'

'I write for Peko Books, Gothic romances. Supermarkets sell them.' Her tone was flat.

'As another writer, you must have known your neighbour fairly well.'

'I knew him. I wouldn't say well. We were writers of . . . different breeds. He was regarded as an artist.' Almost as an afterthought, she added, 'I'm considered a hack.'

Pedersen made no comment. 'Let me ask you, what was your thought when you found him? About what had happened?'

'I thought he was dead, of course. Electricity

14

and water...' She shivered.

'Did you wonder how it happened, how a hair-drier got into the shower with him?'

She shot a quick glance at him. 'I suppose—' her brow puckered—'I guess maybe I thought the hair-drier he kept on the window-sill had fallen in. But how could it have? Wouldn't it just have fallen on the floor?'

'It was his hair-drier? You'd seen it before?'

She nodded. 'One night at a neighbourhood meeting there, someone noticed it in his bathroom. They were teasing him about it. Max was rather—macho. It seemed funny his using a hair-drier. He didn't like being laughed at.'

He nodded. 'We don't. Did he strike you as being suicidal?'

'Odd way to commit suicide.' She gave a ragged sigh and he realized how tightly she was controlling herself. She was more disturbed, had been more shocked, than she was willing to let on. He could tell the effort it took her to continue. 'He was an alcoholic. His wife left him a few years ago and he joined AA. They lived around the corner so I knew him. His wife kept the house and later she remarried. You should talk to her, she'd know if he was suicidal.'

'After the divorce he stayed on in the neighbourhood?'

'Yes. The place next door was for sale, and I suppose he wanted to be near campus. He
15

teaches.' She looked away. 'Taught.'

'He has no children?'

'None I've ever heard of.'

'You say he was an alcoholic.'

'When he first moved in he was drinking. Fairly soon after, he stopped.'

'A pleasant drunk?'

She made an ambiguous gesture. 'It wasn't like that. He held his liquor pretty well, so far as I could see. He was—morose, I guess, more than anything else. When he'd been drinking, I mean.'

'A pleasant neighbour?'

'We didn't have that much to do with each other. We were both working. Max settled down after he stopped drinking so heavily, he had a routine and stuck by it pretty closely.'

'I understand he just finished a book.'

'Yes, after ten years. There's a letdown when you finish a book, but that would hardly have made him suicidal. Now maybe you could call Max paranoid. I'd say that he always was.'

Pedersen straightened a bit in his chair. 'Paranoid?'

'In the popular sense of the word. He—' she hesitated—'I may as well tell you, somebody will, he decided Saturday night that someone was trying to murder him.'

Pedersen waited.

'We were at a party—for him, as a matter of fact. A sort of neighbourhood celebration of his new book.' She paused with an inward

16

expression on her face as though she might be reflecting that her books were not celebrated in such a fashion. 'The party was on a neighbour's deck and the railing alongside the ravine was shaky; she'd warned us to be careful. Max must have leaned against it and knocked it loose. He seemed very shaken for the rest of the evening and later, when we were all walking down the hill together, he said in this ... odd voice that someone had pushed him. None of us believed him.'

But you're wondering now, Pedersen thought. 'And you didn't think that was possible, that he was pushed?'

She sighed. 'Would one of us want to *kill* him?'

'Was he a man who had enemies?'

'Certainly not among the people at that party. Enemies is a strong word. And murder...' She did not go on.

Yes, yes, I know, Pedersen reflected wryly. Murder doesn't happen in a neighbourhood like this—writers, artists, professors. Lady, he thought, you just don't know.

'Assuming,' he said, 'that he had been murdered—of course this is hypothetical—can you think of anyone with sufficient motive for murdering him?'

She shook her head a shade too quickly. 'No one.'

'How about this morning? Did you see anyone over there?'

'No. Only that shower going on and on.'

'Yes. Now tell me about that.'

She sighed again, that same torn sound, and got up to pour two more cups of coffee.

'I'm sorry. We're almost finished.'

'It's all right. It's just that I don't go around finding—'

'I know. This has been a strain for you.'

She shrugged. 'I'm not all that fragile. It's just—well, let's get down to it. Max's alarm must ring around seven-thirty. This morning I was at my sink when his blind went up.'

'Did you greet each other?'

'No. We glanced at each other.'

'And then?'

'There's always a little—interval. I suppose he fills his coffee-maker and plugs it in or something. Then I hear his shower begin.' She nodded towards the open window. 'He never closes his bathroom window.'

He glanced across at the house next door. He could guess that in summer with the windows open like this, sound would travel uninhibited between them. He turned back. 'What time was that?'

'When his shower started? Ten to eight. I looked at the clock before I went to make my bed. I have a routine too, in the morning—I try to be at work by nine. Anyway, I came back and changed the water in the zinnias and went into the living-room to finish picking up. I remember I stopped to watch a jogger going

18

by. Then I came back to the kitchen. Before I get down to writing, I always have a second cup of coffee and do the crossword puzzle. As I was taking down a mug, I glanced at the clock to see how much time I had. It was eight thirty-five. And suddenly it hit me—Max had been showering for forty-eight minutes. He never did that. A panicky feeling swept over me.'

'What did you do?'

'First I called him. I could hear the phone ringing next door but nobody answered. Then it occurred to me that maybe with the shower running, he couldn't hear.'

'At that point, what did you think had happened?'

'I suppose I—I guess I thought he had fallen.'

'And then?'

'I went next door and rang the bell several times. Nobody came. So I—went in.'

'You had a key?'

'No. I turned the knob. The door was open.'

'And?'

'I walked to the bathroom—I kept expecting him to burst out and be furious with me—and knocked. Nobody answered and the shower just went on, so I opened the door. Right away I saw the wire from the wall going over to the tub and I—' she threw him a glance of appeal—'I knew what was wrong.'

'You didn't actually go into the bathroom?'

'No, I had a feeling I'd be electrocuted

too—I guess that doesn't make sense but it was what I felt.'

'And then you called the police.'

'Yes, from Max's phone. That Officer Muller came.'

Pedersen turned the page of his notebook. 'That's very clear. Thank you.' He paused. 'Are you all right?'

She nodded wordlessly.

'Up to answering one more question?'

She nodded again.

'Then I'd like the particulars of that party you mentioned—who was there, where it was held.'

She relaxed a little, as though the move from talk of her discovery of Max's body eased her. But she was reluctant to answer. 'They're just his neighbours, not even close friends.' Her eyes appraised him. 'Do I have to tell you?'

Odd that she should balk over information he could easily obtain. 'Of course not,' he said mildly. 'I'm sure I can get the names from someone else. Of course I'd appreciate your cooperation.'

She frowned, considering. 'All right, I guess it doesn't matter.' She sighed. 'The party was at Leona Morgan's house, up on the hill.'

'The Morgan family that gave all that money to the university?'

'Yes. They're gone now, the parents, and Leona's big interest is the county art museum. She's on the board. Leona was Max's current

... romantic interest.'

'I see. That's Max Follett, Leona Morgan. Who else?'

'There were, let's see, nine of us. The Smiths were there, Florence and Arthur.'

'Now who are they?'

'She's the wife I told you about who left Max. Her husband's a nurseryman. Greengrove Nursery. And there was Max's sister. Her name is Dawn Voletski. She's a potter.' She stopped. 'My God! She doesn't know.'

'I'll get to her right after I finish here. Is Voletski her married name?'

'No, the family anglicized the name. She was Doris Follett, but recently she took back the original name and at the same time changed her first one, too.'

'A legal change?'

'I have no idea. I think after her divorce she just wanted a fresh start. Name and all. It's a little silly, but she's young.' She smiled faintly.

Pedersen nodded. 'My daughter changed her first name when she was in ninth grade. Temporarily, I'm glad to say. So, who else?'

'Did I say Keith and Karin Bloch?'

'No. Tell me about them.'

'Keith teaches ed. psych. at the community college and she makes miniatures.' At Pedersen's inquiring glance, she said, 'Not pictures. These are—well, to me they look like dolls' houses, but I guess they're built to scale

21

and accurate. Right now she's working on a Victorian mansion the art museum is going to use in connection with a fall art show. I think Leona arranged that.'

'With Mr Follett, that's eight.'

'Who did I forget? Oh, Marcie Terpstra. She rents the garage apartment behind the Blochs. Lives there with her little boy and works in the campus bookstore.'

'No husband?'

'No husband. The boy's father's long gone.'

Pedersen took down the addresses. 'I'd better see if I can locate Miss Voletski. You say down the hill on the left?'

She nodded. 'You'll find it. She's painted the door orange.'

He closed his notebook. 'You've been very helpful. You'll be all right now?'

'Of course I will.' The words were abrupt; she was still a bit sullen, resentful of being asked to cooperate with the police. He looked at her, considering. She'd have been about twenty-five in the mid-sixties when the police were 'pigs'. He smiled. The age he had been.

She caught the smile, her face suspicious.

None the less, she politely conducted him to the front door. Outside the world was untroubled. Wheatlike wild oats gilded the hills beyond just as they had done all summer. Above, a fine line of birds unravelled against the sky like a dark thread laid against blue enamel. Beyond Follett's house, the horses had

22

moved to the other end of the field. They formed a bucolic little tableau, the small white horse and the larger dark one a pattern against the glinting green of the meadow.

It was not a scene that suggested murder.

CHAPTER THREE

Karin Bloch put down the tiny piece of wood she was trimming and glanced through the open door of her studio towards the outer door beyond. 'Come,' she called. She was working on the shingled roof of the miniature Victorian house, her first real commission and one she took seriously. As a general rule, no one interrupted her during the morning hours.

It was Marcie. 'Kevin's in the sandbox. Can you walk back with me for a minute, so I can keep my eye on him? I have ... news.'

Karin threw a hungry glance at the table spread with drawings, pots of glue, little stacks of basswood and neat rows of miniature shingles, but she rose and followed Marcie outdoors. 'What's up?' Of all her neighbours, Marcie most rigorously respected her work time. 'Are you all right? You look upset.'

'I am upset. Karin, Max is dead.'

'*Dead? Did you say dead?*'

'Perry just called. She sounded awful.'

'My God, what happened? Did he have a heart attack?' She glanced down at her watch.

'What are you doing here, anyway? Shouldn't Kevin be at the day care centre?'

'They phoned not to bring him. One of the kids came in with a rash and they were trying to reach his mother to take him home. I had to call the store.' She looked towards the sandbox and lowered her voice. 'It wasn't a heart attack. He was electrocuted.'

'*Electrocuted!*'

'He was in the shower and a hair-drier fell in. She found him, Perry did.'

'This gets crazier and crazier. What was Perry doing there while he was showering?'

'I don't know. She sounded so funny I didn't want to ask. The police are there—at Max's, I mean. Some detective interviewed Perry and she had to give all our names, the people at the party Saturday.'

'Why? What does the party have to do with it?'

'Don't ask me. I don't know any more than you do. There must be some reason.'

In the play yard beyond them, Kevin happily sifted sand in large shovelsful from the sandbox to the ground. For the first time it struck Karin that neither of them had expressed regret over the death. 'What a Godawful thing to have happen,' she said. 'He'll never see his new book published.' That, somehow, seemed the loss. Not Max himself but Max never seeing the book, that novel over which he had so laboured, for which he had

24

suffered for so long.

'I know. It's terrible, and it all sounds absolutely crazy. It doesn't seem anybody'd be that careless, having a drier near—' She stopped.

'Yes.' They looked at each other. 'He had it on the bathroom window-sill,' Karin said.

'But if it just fell in the tub, why are the police interested in us? If it was an accident, I mean.'

'Maybe—'

Marcie cut her off, eyes wide. 'Suicide?'

'He was depressed often enough.'

Marcie's face puckered with emotion. 'Do you have ... mixed feelings?'

'What do you mean?'

'Just—I don't know what I feel. Max wasn't my favourite person.'

'He probably wasn't anybody's *favourite* person.'

'Leona. He was hers, certainly. And Dawn's. Lots of people liked Max.'

Karin smiled faintly. 'Well, even though Max was hard to take at times, I doubt that anyone'll be glad he's dead.'

'Not his publisher, certainly. Or—'

'My God! I wonder if Dawn knows.'

Marcie looked stricken. 'I *never* thought. How could I not? I was just so—'

'Let me call Perry and ask. You keep an eye on Kevin.' She left Marcie looking after her, her face anxious.

On the eighth ring, the receiver was picked

25

up.

'It's Karin. Marcie told me. Has anyone gone down to talk to Dawn, do you know?'

'That policeman. I should go, but I'm afraid I'd upset her more. I'm sort of—shaky.'

'Of course. It must have been a terrible shock. Look, Perry, why don't we go down together? I can get Dawn to come up to the house with me. She shouldn't be there alone.'

'No, you're right. What about Florence?'

'She has Arthur. Are you OK, Perry? Are you up to this?'

'Everything feels a little unreal, but otherwise I guess I'm all right. I'll meet you out front on the road.' The plan of action had a salutary effect on Perry. Her voice more normal, she added, 'Tell Marcie we'll talk later in the week about the writing. She brought some of her poetry for me to look at—that's why I called her, so she'd know not to come by today.'

Karin hung up. This was the first she had heard of Marcie's writing poetry, or for that matter, anything else. The morning had been full of news.

CHAPTER FOUR

Approaching the house, Pedersen spotted the crisp oblong of strong colour. The rest of the building had not seen a brush in years. Well-

26

proportioned, it must once have been a handsome structure in the Eastlake style of the area, but the long droughts and lashing winter rains had long since stripped it of any small elegance to which it laid claim. With its flaked and blistered paint, the house had an air of desiccation. The gate in the fence that enclosed it leaned tiredly and opened with a rasping sigh.

The cramped little basement windows had also been curtained in orange. Together, the bright door and cheerful curtains lent a touch of gallantry to the whole. He sighed. In a matter of moments his message would cast a shadow over these efforts at light-heartedness.

He rang the doorbell and then slid his left hand into his jacket pocket and ran the jade worry beads through his fingers. He had bought them when he and Freda visited Greece and carried them ever since. At moments like these, he found them a solace. After a short time he could hear someone mounting the steps inside.

A small, sturdy-looking young woman wearing a denim skirt and sandals, with tights and a turtleneck shirt of bright blue and an enveloping apron, opened the door gingerly with one clay-coated hand. She had dark eyes, high colour and a tangle of brown curls. 'Oh,' she said, 'I thought—I'll wash.' She stopped as though it had occurred to her that she should question this presence.

27

'Miss Voletski?'

'Yes.' She said it tentatively as though it might be the wrong answer.

'Detective Pedersen.' He flipped open his identification folder.

Abruptly her attention focused on him. He was used to the stillness that gripped people to whom he announced himself.

'I need to speak to you. May I come in?'

She turned and led him into the hall and down the stairs. When she turned, her face was frightened.

'Better sit down,' he said gently.

'I—I'll wash my hands.' She turned and left the room. A moment later he heard water running.

She was postponing the moment. He looked around. A grey kitten, already half cat, was curled on the sofa-bed. The kitchen end of the large room had been partitioned off by open shelves as a cooking and work area. A large crock stood to one side, covered closely by a wet cloth, a potter's wheel occupied a small table, and on the shelves jars of glaze and various finished and partially finished pots were set. It appeared she had not yet arrived at a personal style: several finished pieces were conventional in form, bowls or vases such as he might have picked up in any shop on the mall. Others, apparently more recent, showed the first attempts at originality. He was sure his wife Freda, who had once taken a ceramics course and was more knowledgeable than he about such things, would agree they were, so far, not successful. One, still unglazed, was so wildly amorphous in shape that Pedersen doubted it would hold water. Another was boxlike with squared corners; even in his ignorance Pedersen felt sure it would present problems in the firing and would leak at the seams. The one on which she had been working seemed to be patterned after a gourd. There was something childishly appealing in the oddly assorted collection.

A door opened and she came back into the room drying her hands on a white towel. The frightened look was still on her face. 'It's my brother,' she said, 'isn't it? There isn't ... anyone else.'

He waited for her to sit down. 'Yes,' he said, 'I'm afraid it is.'

She leaned forward. 'He's hurt? Not—'

'He's been killed, Miss Voletski. Instantly, it couldn't have been more than a second or two.'

Her face was slack and she let out a little exhalation of breath. The kitten, as though in response, stirred and then jumped into her lap.

He answered the question she didn't ask. 'He was apparently electrocuted—a hair-drier. He was showering.'

Her face began to crumple.

'Here,' he said impotently, 'let me have the towel.'

When the knock came and he saw her off with her neighbours, it was with relief. Walking back up the road towards the Follett house, he reflected on their conversation. She had been able to tell him nothing. She had never thought her brother suicidal. She knew of no one with whom he had had recent difficulty. No change had taken place in his life save the finishing of the book.

'There was a party to celebrate that,' he said. She nodded without words. By the time Perry Devane and her neighbour appeared, he had decided this was cruelty, trying to question her at this moment. Despite the valiant orange curtains, the dark-eyed girl struck him as defenceless, completely and utterly defenceless.

* * *

Back at Max Follett's house, he found a bustle of activity. The crime scene investigators, the coroner's deputy and Detective Ronald Tate were fully occupied.

Tate was surveying Follett's study. 'What a mess,' he said as Pedersen came in. By Tate's standards it was a mess; Pedersen, himself not compulsive when it came to tidiness, thought it looked normally, even comfortably, disordered.

'Did you alert the team? Tell them to treat it as a murder till we know more?'

'I did. I also told them to be extremely careful that nothing is carried off without meticulous documentation and to take *nothing* they don't have to. These materials—' Tate waved a hand—'will probably go to a library.'

'Good. I've told the sister. I think I'll just hie myself up the hill to see the hostess of that party before word gets all over town that Follett's dead. Will you hang around here for a while, keep track of things?'

'The *Banner*'s already been here. I told them he'd had an accident, that we'd have details later.'

'Good,' Pedersen said again. It was what he would have said. He and Ronald Tate had worked together long enough to have learned each other well.

He walked briskly around the corner to where the road began to climb. Despite the steady rain of the day before, the surface beneath his feet was almost dry. That morning there had been no fog to burn off and the sun was moving higher, warming his face. It appeared summer was settling back into its predictable pattern.

Gradually he slowed his stride, taking in what he saw. The neighbourhood had retained vestiges of its original pastoral character but now here and there raw new buildings stood, looking undressed without any of the robust foliage that surrounded the older houses. The original planning had been poorly done—he thought of the proximity of the Follett and Devane houses despite their wide flanking fields—but building had been sparse enough to lend a carelessness to the neighbourhood. The weathered houses and small pastures, the tiny graveyard, the occasional dips in the road, the little creek that ducked under an old bridge and the horses grazing close by it, together created a scene that recalled the Bay Cove of his boyhood. The medicinal tang of eucalyptus was in his nostrils. As he climbed, the feathery trees thinned and across the meadows he could catch sight of the bay. Ahead to his left a large house was set at the highest point on a broad tract of land. As he drew closer to it, he could see that beyond the house the bay glittered in the morning sun.

From this side there was no sign of the deck with the broken railing, although he caught a glimpse of an outside staircase towards the back. The house was broad-eaved and in a subtle way Japanese in feeling. He rang the doorbell.

It took one glance for Pedersen to understand Max Follett's interest in the woman who opened the door. Being chosen by Leona Morgan would have affirmed any man's sense of virility. She was slender but richly curved, with gleaming, densely black hair pulled back from a face so creamy she might never have stepped into the California sun.

She stirred under his gaze. 'Yes?'

'Mrs Morgan?'

'Miss. Yes.'

He identified himself. 'Could I come in and talk with you for a few minutes?'

She raised both hands, letting them slide back over the smoothness of the dark hair that was drawn into a firm twist at her nape. 'Talk with me? About what?' She frowned. But she stepped aside for him to enter.

She led him to a study on the left. On a huge slablike desk, papers, letters and ledgers testified to the fact that she had been working. 'Museum,' she said with an air of dismissal; she seemed to take for granted that her work was known. She waved him to one of a pair of deep leather chairs. 'Now. What's this all about?'

'It's about a neighbour and friend of yours, Max Follett.'

Something darted in her eyes. She waited.

'He's had an accident.'

'He's all right? I mean—'

'No, he isn't all right.' He chose his words. 'I'm afraid he was killed.'

'Oh no! Oh my God!' After a barely perceptible pause she shook her head. 'I always told him he drove like a maniac.'

A natural assumption, thought Pedersen. Or were they merely cleverly chosen words to show her innocence of the real cause of death?

'It wasn't an auto accident,' he said. He did not explain further, but went directly to his question. 'I'm here because I understand on Saturday you gave a party for Mr Follett.'

Her hands went up to her head again. An interesting mannerism. Did she do that when she was feeling unsure? Out of control?

'I don't understand,' she said. 'Why do you want to know about that?'

Pedersen had not expected that she would let the topic of Follett's death drop like that. 'I understand the party was for Mr Follett and that there was some sort of incident during it.'

'Oh.' Her face told him nothing. 'You mean the railing? Max leaned against it. I hadn't realized it was loose till after the party started. Then I noticed it seemed shaky, so I warned everyone. Keith says it's termite damage.'

'Anything else?'

She was beginning to look uneasy. 'I'm not sure what you mean. It started to rain. It never rains in summer, and we certainly never have thunderstorms, but we did Saturday night. But you know that. Is that what you mean?'

'I mean anything out of the ordinary.' He waited. She said nothing. 'Who came to this party?'

'Just neighbours, people from right around here. It wasn't a big affair, but I tried to make it festive, especially festive, I mean, since it was such a special occasion.' She stopped suddenly. 'Does Dawn know?'

'Yes. I was just down there. She's a friend of yours?'

'Yes.' She looked past him. 'She was here yesterday. She came out in all that rain with zucchini, just because she'd said she'd bring some. She dropped some off at Max's and Perry's, too.' She sighed. 'That must have been the last time she saw him.'

'Miss Morgan, may I ask you a personal question? Were you just a neighbour or perhaps a—more special, let's say intimate, friend of Max Follett's?'

Without warning, the façade crumbled. She put a hand over her mouth and, without speaking, nodded. Her eyes swam with tears.

'This must be very sad news for you, then, but I do need someone to tell me something about Mr Follett. Maybe you'll do that. Most of us in the town know only the public man—I hardly have to tell you he was one of our most notable citizens.'

She nodded again. 'What happened?'

He had waited for her to ask. 'It appears to have been some sort of—' he hesitated— 'accident, a hair-drier falling into the tub while he was showering.'

'Then he wasn't—' She caught herself.

'Yes? Wasn't?'

She looked at her hands. 'Responsible. But of course if it was carelessness, he was responsible.'

Pedersen wondered if it had been the word

35

responsible she had been about to utter or if the word was murdered. He said, 'Tell me about Mr Follett.'

She sighed. 'He was a complicated, difficult, rather unhappy man. It wasn't easy having a close relationship with Max. He was rather ... engulfing, but he himself didn't want to commit.'

'Commit? You mean commit himself to the relationship?'

'Yes. He wanted to come and go as he chose and—' she added with more fire—'with whom he chose, but he expected you—me, that is—to be here whenever the spirit moved him to see me.'

'That must have been hard to tolerate.'

'Oh—' she tossed her head and then the anxious hands checked the hair—'I didn't tolerate it. We weren't getting on at all. Not, of course, that I want to think of him—dead.' She gave a nervous little giggle. 'You know, just then I thought: He'll be in a real rage at not seeing the book published. People think strange things at a time like this.' She paused. 'Have you talked to Florence Smith yet?'

He looked at her closely. 'No. Why do you ask?'

'Oh ...' She seemed unsure as to whether or not to go on.

'Something occurred to you.'

'Just—well, I saw them, not exactly together, Saturday. I thought that was pretty

36

strange.'

'Not *exactly* together?'

'I was standing in the Cheese Store waiting my turn, when I glanced across the street and saw Florence come out of the Saltcellar—that's a little coffee shop. About two minutes later Max came out. That isn't a place most of our friends go, it's more a teenage hangout, so it occurred to me that Florence and Max must be having an—'

He smiled. 'Assignation?'

'Well, a meeting of some sort. Maybe she'll know something about what Max was up to.'

'You don't.'

'Not lately. We haven't seen much of each other for a week or two. Once for dinner, that's all.'

He nodded. 'Back to the party. Was Mr Follett upset or frightened at his near accident?'

'Yes, he was frightened. Out of proportion, in fact. We all went in then, it had started raining, and he was very quiet, very shaken, all the rest of the evening.'

'Did he say anything?'

'About his accident? No.'

'You started to say you planned to—what?'

She looked confused. 'Oh. We had decided not to see each other—' she looked down—'as lovers, any longer. Actually, I decided it.'

'But you weren't angry with him. You liked him well enough to give a party for him.'

37

'That had been planned for weeks. Besides, we were still friends. Everyone was delighted that Max had finished his book. We all went through those birth pains.' She laughed.

'I understand he used to drink.'

'Not since I've known him. Florence would know about that.'

'He wasn't a violent drunk?'

She gave an impatient little shrug. 'So far as I knew, he wasn't a drunk at all. Ask Florence.' After a moment she went on. 'I don't mean he was perfect. As I told you, he wasn't. He'd probe and probe until he found out the one thing you'd rather people didn't know and then he'd keep referring to it so only you and he knew what he was talking about. Or so you hoped. But he could be charming, too. I suppose the inquisitiveness was just part of being a writer.'

'And there's nothing else you can tell me about that party? How about conversational exchanges? Anything worth paying attention to, anything you especially remember?'

'No. Really not. Talk about writing and people we knew. Politics, zucchini recipes— Dawn's a big gardener—and, oh, I don't know, even about TV. Nothing special.'

She was not going to tell him voluntarily; he would have to ask. 'Did Mr Follett think he was pushed against the rail?'

She laughed, a nervous crescendo. 'Did someone say that?'

'Someone did.'

'Max was paranoid, but not that paranoid. Nobody would *push* him.'

'Just suppose someone had. Who would be your nomination for pusher?'

'What a question.' Again the artificial laugh. 'You're asking me to say one of my guests had lethal intentions. I won't nominate anyone.'

Pedersen rose. 'You're right, it isn't a question a hostess, or a friend, could answer. I would like to take a look at that deck, though, if you don't mind.'

The deck was off the cathedral-ceilinged living-room, through sliding doors. Because of the house's plan, open, with the dining-room and kitchen raised a few steps above the living-room, the expanse of sun-gilded bay was visible from the entire area. The deck itself was wide and at this hour sunny and welcoming, despite the ragged rent in the bayside railing. Pausing, Pedersen laid a hand on a lounge chair. It would be good to stop right here, take off his jacket, lie back on one of these long canvas chairs and let the sun melt away all the tensions, the thoughts of unfinished paperwork, of the unmown lawn awaiting him at home, of Freda's uncharacteristically angry words the night before as she complained that he was present only in body, forever preoccupied with a case, especially when she had a problem.

He removed his hand from the chair. There

was still a good deal to do back at the Follett house. On the way home that night, he'd pick up a pot of those painted daisies Freda liked, to let her know that, although his work was often on his mind at home, it was she who was on his mind during the long days. She didn't know how often. He was, as she sometimes told him in teasing, a uxorious man.

'Just how did the accident happen?' he asked.

'Well, we were sitting around, talking, eating, drinking. The sky looked threatening but we had no idea the rain would come in the way it did. Absolutely without warning there was this great splatter of raindrops and the next minute it started hard. The place was in chaos—we were all scurrying here and there rescuing food and cushions and sweaters, nobody paying any attention to anyone else, trying to get the things and ourselves inside fast. In the middle of it all, Max gave this funny shrill scream and grabbed at Arthur and crumpled forward on the deck. I suppose his clutching Arthur that way is what saved him. Several of us turned to help him up and as we did, with this sort of ... groan, the broken railing just tumbled into the ravine below.' She shivered.

Pedersen stood visualizing the scene. In those circumstances a shove might well be accidental. What was interesting was Follett's assumption that it was intentional. Was it his

40

'paranoia'? Or, he wondered, was it that Max Follett had found out one uncomfortable secret too many and he knew it?

CHAPTER FIVE

Rounding the corner on his return from the hill, Pedersen could see the tall lean figure of Ronald Tate standing squarely before the Follett house, scrutinizing it. With his wire-rimmed glasses and corduroy jacket, he could have been taken for a sociologist down from campus doing research into the odd and wonderful ways of the local natives. Pedersen joined him.

'I've been thinking,' Tate said. 'If it is murder, the question is, could someone have got in without the interested Miss Devane noticing?' He turned to Pedersen. 'There's a little path down in back, though even that's not totally concealed by shrubbery. She could probably see anyone leaving by the front door, especially if he walked back to the main road—he'd have to go right past her. But what if it were someone she's used to seeing arrive and for that reason never noticed? His sister? A girlfriend?'

'The milkman. The iceman.' Pedersen smiled. 'Life is tough, nothing's delivered to the house any more. Cuts down on suspects.'

Tate nodded. 'Come see this path.'

Slightly overgrown, it wound off down the hill towards the main road, a little path children might have made taking a short cut. Behind the Follett and Devane houses it passed at an angle, partly masked from view by sprawling eunoymous vines. 'See?' Tate said. 'Someone could have come up by this path and then cut across the backyard to the side door. I asked the team to check the area but it seems the ground cover is too springy to take a footprint. And everything dried fast after that rain, the ground was so thirsty.'

They turned back to the house. 'I've been talking to his girlfriend—one of them, anyway,' Pedersen said. 'Trying to find out about his being pushed against the railing. I didn't learn a hell of a lot.' He frowned. 'We'd better talk to his former wife, though.'

Back in the house, the crime scene team was working room by room. The living-room had again taken on its air of drowsy neglect—couch pulled slightly askew before the fireplace, cushions piled at one end where someone, presumably Follett, had lain reading or perhaps looking into a rainy day fire. Sunday newspapers were scattered nearby. Chairs bore indentations that could have come from the day before or the week before; it appeared the room was not often subjected to a thorough going-over. The curtains, still drawn, shielded the room from the light of noonday. On a little table a sticky-looking glass had been placed in a plastic bag preparatory to being taken away; on it, Pedersen could still see the dust from fingerprinting. Probably Dawn's from the Sunday visit.

Pedersen turned into the study. 'We should check out Follett's papers, see if there's anything right at hand that might bear on this.'

Max Follett's papers could not be said to be in order nor was there anything resembling a suicide note among them. A check with the technicians confirmed that nothing had been removed. Old letters from his editor, a note from his agent, a request to speak at the university women's club, three invitations with RSVPs (Pedersen wondered if Follett had been the sort of man who bothered to respond), paid and unpaid bills, a Rollidex address file, several bank statements apparently not checked for errors in envelopes crammed with cheques, scribbled-upon pages from an old manuscript, a notebook filled with barely legible jottings related to his writing. Nothing that readily revealed anything pertinent to the death.

A large looseleaf calendar that presented a month at a time showed a notation for the Saturday night party and another unspecified one for the same Saturday marked merely '12.15'. The week to come showed entries for speaking engagements, one on campus and one in town, and a 'U meeting'. Among the papers readily at hand there was no copy of his manuscript. And no will; probably that was in a safe-deposit box.

Pedersen walked through to the kitchen and stood looking out of the window at the Devane house. 'I wonder why that door was unlocked,' he said. 'A paranoid man. You know, Ron—' He stopped.

'Yes, Carl?'

'You know, this is a little world unto itself, this neighbourhood. I've heard of them. Down in town they call them the Art Gang.'

'It doesn't sound like a term of endearment.'

'No, but not derogatory, either. Just descriptive. I've been thinking. We have to ask the right questions. If we ask the wrong ones, I have a feeling they'll draw together and protect each other.'

'You make them sound like a ring of covered wagons. Does that make us the Indians?'

Pedersen smiled. 'Not exactly. But we have to learn what they are, this Art Gang. Who is who. I think we have to proceed carefully with the bunch that went to the Saturday night party.' In a sudden lightening of mood, he swung around. 'How about lunch when they're finished here?'

*   *   *

Because lunch was a break before what would probably be a long, hard afternoon of work, they treated themselves to the local Chinese restaurant, which had a reputation for excellent food.

'Freda,' commented Pedersen over his broccoli and black mushrooms, 'tells me if I ever take to coming home regularly for lunch, she'll divorce me.'

'Maybe that was my trouble.' Tate's smile was wry.

'How long is it now? You must have got used to being by yourself.'

'You never get used to it. Oh, it has some good features. You make all your own plans and decisions. You don't waste a lot of energy over pointless discussions. But there's no one, no . . .'

'Significant Other?'

'Damned straight. That's it exactly. I have great respect these days for that term.' He paused. 'I guess I've never told you what happened with me and my wife. Not that there's much to tell.'

'Don't if you don't want to.'

'I don't mind.' He looked down at his plate. 'She was quite a bit younger. We met at a party the week she dropped out of college. She'd got in with a bunch who were into everything. Pot, booze, meth, coke, you name it. She couldn't get through a day without some sort of help. But we had something going, it seemed very good to me. Finally she saw it was either me or her junk. Not both. I think she really wanted out of that life, and I can be pretty uncompromising. It was tough for her—hell,

45

for both of us—but by the time she was done, she had kicked everything. After we were married we had a couple of really good years—four, actually. She went back to school and was really excited about her work. Then she decided to go on to graduate school. After that, she outgrew me.'

'Come on, Ron. You're not that easily outgrown.'

'Maybe not. What happened was that she didn't *need* me any longer. That's what it really was. At a certain point in her life somebody like me—straight, a police detective even—well, it was as though she used me till she got free of all her hang-ups. What would the psychologists say that made me, her superego?'

Pedersen laughed. 'I think it's more complicated than that.'

'She used to ridicule me, made fun of me for not even smoking cigarettes—she never did give that up—but she wanted someone like me. Somebody who would put his foot down and say either-or to her.'

'What's she doing now?'

'She's at Berkeley, working on a doctorate. I think she's living with some law student.' He grinned. 'Same principle, but a step up.'

'You're divorced?'

'Oh, it's been final for quite a while now. Took me a little time to get over it, but I am now.'

Pedersen reached for the teapot. 'I'm glad

you told me. I've wondered.'

Ronald Tate smiled. 'There's not much you don't know about me. I always think of myself as all too transparent.'

'An open book?'

'An open book.' He smiled.

Pedersen pushed his plate away and sat back contentedly. 'Well, I just wish this Follett thing were a little more like that. It looks to me as though it may be a tightly-closed book, an uncut volume. And I think—' he grinned—'we just may have trouble cutting the pages free.'

CHAPTER SIX

Arthur Smith liked to come home for lunch. As a child he had had to watch the other children filing off at noon to their respective houses while he stayed behind to eat with the sons and daughters of working mothers or chronically busy ones. His mother was ill. In later life he learned the nature of her illness, but as a child he knew only that she spent whole days closeted in her room, shades drawn, unwilling to be disturbed. Occasionally she emerged, moving out of her room slowly, head down, to sit tiredly with Arthur and his father and toy with the meal her husband had prepared. Sometimes they quarrelled, or rather, his father shouted at her. But for the most part his childhood home remained in Arthur's mind a hushed place of darkness, unease, tension.

Florence understood—and welcomed him at lunch-time.

At two minutes to one he arrived. His punctuality was so reliable that Florence was drawing the quiche from the oven as she heard his car pull into the driveway. He came in, one arm full of irises, great plump bronze blossoms.

'Arthur! Where did they come from?' Arthur's nursery sold no cut flowers.

'I saw them on my way to work, right down the road in that vacant field. I stopped to pick them before someone else did and kept them in water all morning. I'll show you the place, must be the site of an old garden. Remember when I found tulips this spring?'

'Oh, there. Yes, I remember.' Florence fished a vase down from the top shelf of the cupboard and filled it with water at the kitchen sink. 'Sit down,' she called. 'It's all ready but dressing the salad.' She paused. 'You heard?'

His answer was slightly muffled; he had dropped a napkin. 'Terrible. A shaver or something fell in the tub.'

'A hair-drier.' She returned to set the flowers at one end of the table. 'He was showering. Karin says the police are all over the place.'

'Ironic, just as he finished the book.'

'Everybody says that—Marcie called, and Leona. Dawn's at the Blochs'. I went over. Poor kid.'

Arthur raised his eyebrows.

'Well, poor woman, then. She didn't have anyone else.'

'How's she taking it?'

'Marcie says Karin's being wonderful with her. You know Karin, she should have had *ten* kids.'

Arthur rose and turned to the serving table; he began to dress the salad. His back to her, he said. 'How about you? Are you upset?'

'Of course, everybody is, but no more than if—I mean...'

He turned back to her, his eyes intent. 'You seem surprisingly undisturbed.' He sat down again.

'Of course I'm disturbed, but I've told you twenty times if I've told you once, Max has been out of my life for six years and that's that.'

He began to eat silently.

An edge of exasperation crept into her voice. 'Certainly *now* you're not going to be jealous?'

'I was never jealous.'

'Whatever you call it, then.'

He took another mouthful of quiche. 'Have you seen Max to talk to lately?'

'Salt. I forgot it.' She got up and went into the kitchen. 'Saturday night at the party. You know that,' she said from the other room. She returned. 'This quiche needs more seasoning.'

'It's fine. Come sit down.' He studied the face across from him. 'Just Saturday night?'

'When else would I have?' Her eyes did not

49

meet his. 'Here, have some.' She pushed the salt and pepper towards him. 'I won't commit suicide if you add salt. Isn't that what the chef of some French emperor did?' She stopped. 'I guess that's not the best lunch-table topic right now.'

'What does that mean? Did the police say Max killed himself?'

'Apparently they asked Dawn a lot of questions that suggested he might have.'

'Now? With the book done?' Arthur shook his head. 'That's an interesting thought.'

He finished his lunch in silence. Finally Florence spoke. 'What are you thinking?'

'I'm thinking about Max as a suicide. How was Leona?'

'Shaken, I think. I've never heard her sound like that. Nervous. None of the usual airy self-confidence. I never did understand their relationship anyway, so it's hard to tell what she feels.'

'I thought it was perfectly obvious.'

'What was?'

'That they were sleeping together, had a thing going.'

'Oh, that.' She was impatient. 'I mean, was there a real relationship or was it just an occasional roll in the hay? They never talked about living together and certainly not about marriage. Besides, I thought lately he had his eye on Marcie.'

Arthur put his fork down with a clink.

'*Marcie!* Her too? He wouldn't—'

'Why wouldn't he? She's darling. Any man would lust after her.' She laughed. 'Why not Max?'

'But she's so—'

'Young? Innocent? She's had one child out of wedlock, as we used to say, she was married to—or living with—a man who was a real disaster.' At his face she repeated it. 'A disaster, yes, that's what Kevin's father was. That's why she threw him out. She's a lovely young woman, I grant you, but she's not all that innocent. She's told me about some of the boys she's known.'

Arthur stood up, his face, usually so gentle, rigid with anger. 'Boys, maybe. But I can't see her with Max, not that randy, bottom-pinching, lecherous—'

Florence laughed in a sudden release of tension. 'Arthur, I don't think I've ever heard you say anything like that. Come on, he didn't do anything to her, he just looked, I'm sure. Maybe tried. Besides, why does that upset you so?'

He continued to look at her coldly.

Her smile faded. 'You aren't angry about Marcie, are you? It's me. You've been acting peculiar all weekend. Ever since Saturday.'

'I don't know what you're talking about,' said Arthur icily. 'But I will tell you one thing. I'm not sorry to see the last of Max. I'm *glad* the bastard's dead.'

After he had left the room she remained in her chair, silent. Finally she rose and began to clear the table. Passing the mirror above the sideboard, she caught a glimpse of herself, the pretty pointed face anxious. What was it Max had called it? Pinched. She thought: I look guilty. I should have told Arthur about meeting Max Saturday, told him in an offhand way so I'd have deflected his suspicions. But Max was being so sweet when I left him—and Max's bark is always worse than his bite. I didn't think he'd tell Arthur we'd met.

In a moment of sudden self-hate, she thought: It's true, all those things Max always said to me. I do talk—even think—in clichés. I am denying, manipulative, even with a wonderful man like Arthur. I can't ... I can't ... She began to cry, for Max, for herself, for Arthur, and because the only way her mind would finish the thought was with the words 'find a way to happiness'.

CHAPTER SEVEN

Leona had been unable to eat lunch. Alone on her deck, the chair turned so her back was to the broken railing, she forced herself to sit still and try to make sense of the things that had happened to her in the past weeks. She no longer had the impulse to cry; it was as if not Max but something in her had died. She was numb, empty. Totally removed. The whole experience could have happened to someone else, a character in a novel she had read. She felt only this terrible restlessness. No emotion.

She knew, she had always known, why Max wanted her. The things he had said to her on that awful night and all that had happened in the weeks since had only underscored her knowledge. In all their two years it had been only in rare moments that he had allowed himself to relate to anything in her other than the surface, the way she looked, the way in which the community regarded her. Yet she had permitted their relationship to continue. She still did not understand it. Was it that she too had connected only with the surface: Max Follett, acclaimed novelist? She had never allowed herself to wonder long, yet her behaviour with him had been different from that with any other man she had known. And certainly she had never before—but no. That she would not think about.

The tranquillizer she had taken to ease her tension—she had been so jumpy she could barely stay still—was wearing off. A psychiatrist had once told her she internalized her problems. 'Let some of it out,' he had advised. 'Nobody will die.' Thinking of that now, she wanted to laugh.

She rose and went into the house. Sun spilled through the broad windows of the raised dining area and over the surface of the long walnut table. It had been her family's table—in fact, more things than not in the house had been her family's—and to Leona it was familiar beyond being seen. This morning, however, the sun unearthed buried ruddy lights and set the wood aglow; it caught even her eye. For a moment, something in her throat made her swallow. The house was lovely, yet in the midst of the loveliness that was her home, she felt only this terrible desolation, hollowness. Perhaps she had loved Max more than she thought, despite all that had happened.

She stopped pacing and walked to the window. The neighbourhood had changed since she was a little girl. When her father had moved there two years before she was born, the road and hillside were almost unpopulated. His thirty acres and the two big properties alongside them where the university now crouched against the highest hills had been pasture with redwoods beyond.

Things didn't look too different now. The university had preserved the old stone barn, kept the pastureland with a few cattle grazing, and scattered its several small colleges out of sight among the redwood forests. But there was change in the town. Filled parking lots. Long supermarket lines. Traffic jams on the freeway. Streets to be avoided alone late at night. Locks on everything. Security systems. Except for those things, Leona liked the changes. And now that the art museum was firmly established, she found herself more and more involved with people who interested her.

Including the Art Gang. She wasn't sure how the term had arisen. They had appeared, a handful of artists and artisans, one by one buying up property that was being subdivided, telling others like themselves, building houses and studios and workshops and settling in—potters, writers, a weaver, a glassblower, an actor, a sculptor.

She had begun pacing again, so nervous she had the sensation that small things were crawling over her skin.

The bunch at her place Saturday night had not been Art Gang people—oh, some of them qualified, all right, but she regarded them in a different way, as neighbours. But for her only one of the group had ever stood out: Max. Having him in the neighbourhood was like having Mailer or Bellow; everyone knew who he was, he was forever being interviewed and had an audience of literate readers waiting for him to give them another important book. She had known he would, too. Just being around Max was full of promise.

But promise was the word. It had always been only promise. She had waited for things to move a little, patient at first. Then she tried being offended. Making him jealous. Ignoring him. Finally she had moved to ultimatums. At one point she felt she had reached a state where all he would have to do was—what, whistle? That was about it.

She had to get out of the house. Thinking of Max had done this to her. The two years dragging on, hope immediately crushed by a kind of despair, then hope again, had left its mark on her. And then, she couldn't believe it herself—

The telephone rang. A wave of relief washed over her as she turned from her thoughts and walked briskly to her desk.

CHAPTER EIGHT

'First,' said Pedersen, as they picked up their checks and prepared to leave the restaurant, 'we see Florence Smith. Then I think we should look at the rest of that bunch who were at the party, just to get the feel of things, how they relate to each other and to Follett. I'd like you with me, Ron.'

Tate nodded. Pedersen relied on him for the details of paperwork, the taking of statements, the tracking down of hard-to-find suspects, all the small but not incidental aspects of organizing evidence. But the discussion of a case was essential, too. That was where they did most of the real thinking through of a case.

'So,' said Pedersen, as they paid their checks, 'we start with the former wife.'

The former wife had been crying, and she greeted them with a resigned air, as though she had known she could not evade their eventual visit. Small, fair-haired, tending towards scrawniness and with the first hints on her worried little face of the woman she would be in later years, she was still pretty. She evoked in Pedersen a tenderness: his impulse was to reassure rather than to question her.

Although she submitted to his interrogation with a sort of pained passivity, most of what she told him was not helpful. Max abusive? Violent? No, he 'said things' when he was drinking, but he drank no longer. She couldn't imagine anyone's wanting to push him, although at times, like all wives, she'd have happily murdered him. Here she giggled uneasily. But, she hastened to add, he had no real enemies. And Max could be—

'Charming?' offered Pedersen, recalling Leona's words.

'Yes, when he wanted to he could be—I guess that's the word, charming.'

'And you?' Pedersen asked. 'Did you still have a—relationship.'

'Oh, when you've been married for seven years, you still feel connected,' she answered vaguely.

'An amicable relationship?'

'Amicable?' She looked from Pedersen to

Tate. 'Yes, I suppose it was amicable.' She considered. 'You know, with Max and Arthur it was like night and day. Arthur's a wonderful man. He has such courage.' She glanced shyly at Ronald Tate, who had not spoken during the visit. 'Courage is the word for Arthur. I'm so lucky, and sometimes I forget and abuse my relationship with him.'

'Oh?' said Pedersen. 'In what way?'

She was vague. 'In ways.'

'I see. When did you last see Max Follett?'

She seemed surprised. 'At the party Saturday night.'

'And before that?'

'Before that? What do you mean?'

'You were both seen coming out of a coffee house Saturday.'

Alarm touched her face and was gone. She said, 'No.'

'No? You mean you weren't there?'

'I don't remember being in a coffee house Saturday.'

She wasn't a total innocent. She understood about not remembering what she didn't wish to discuss. 'You're quite sure?'

Her eyes met his, steady. 'Sure.'

She would not back down now. As he rose to leave, he said, 'You said your husband and Max Follett were like day and night. In what way was Follett like night?'

She laughed nervously. 'I meant our relationships were—different. Everything's so

58

easy with Arthur. He's consistent. I know where I'm at with him.'

He remembered. 'Mrs Smith, did you think of Max Follett as a suicidal man?'

'Max?' She laughed with a certain bitterness. 'Never. Never. That's one thing Max would never do, kill '

*   *   *

Keith Bloch answered the door, an amiable giant with a sheaf of papers in one hand, a pen in the other. He led the two men into the living-room and laid the papers on the table. 'I came home to do some work. My office was a madhouse today. There's something about summer school.'

'And now here we are, interrupting you,' Pedersen said. 'We won't be long. Just want to ask a couple of questions about Max Follett. Is your wife here, too?'

'Karin's in the studio with Dawn. You want me to get her?'

'Not right now.' They took the chairs he had waved them towards.

Lowering his voice slightly, Bloch said, 'I don't know a hell of a lot about Max. I may not be much help.'

'But you were friendly enough to meet now and then, as you did Saturday at the party Miss Morgan gave?'

'Oh yes. And Max dropped by from time to

time.'

'What impression did you have of him?'

He grinned. 'You really want to know? Abrasive. Provocative. I think basically he was a pretty frustrated guy.'

'Frustrated?'

'Yes.'

'You mean because it took him so long to write his second book?' Tate asked.

'That too, but I meant frustrated over women.'

'Women were his major problem?' Pedersen said.

'One of them, certainly. Four bouts with marriage and God knows how many other— arrangements, and still he was a loner. And he did seem to be suffering from writer's block, too. Ten years between books is a long time.' He laughed. 'Not that I didn't empathize. One reason I teach at the community college is that I'm damned if I'll get on that publish or perish treadmill. Writing has never been my favourite activity.' He glanced at the papers. 'It doesn't appear to be my students', either.'

'To get back to Follett.'

'Yes. All I know is that Max was a man of many problems.' He looked uneasily towards the door. 'I hope they can't hear me in the studio. Dawn would never forgive me.'

'She liked her brother, I gather.'

'Yes, she did. And he was all the family she had. He was twelve years older, probably
60

seemed a little like a parent. This is hard on her.'

'It must be. What about this party Saturday night?'

'What about it?'

'Didn't Mr Follett have an accident? Or a near miss?'

'Oh, that. Yes. He leaned on a railing we'd just discovered was shaky. I suggested Leona barricade it, but she didn't want to spoil the way the place looked. She warned everyone.'

'You're sure he leaned on it?'

'Oh, you've been told Max thought someone pushed him. That was just Max. No one pushed him.'

'You're sure?'

Keith Bloch turned his head from one detective to the other. 'Max Follett's death was no accident. Is that what this is all about?'

'We just don't know yet. That's what we're trying to find out.'

'I see.' Bloch studied their faces.

Pedersen smiled and stood up. 'I wonder if we could leave you to your papers and join the women in the studio?'

Puzzlement crossed Keith Bloch's face. 'Sure. But if you want to talk, I can bring Karin out here.'

Pedersen waved a hand dismissively. 'I have a soft spot for workshops. I do some cabinetwork in spare moments. In fact, Detective Tate likes studios, too.'

61

Bloch's face changed. 'What sort of cabinetwork? I do that kind of thing too, I love to work with my hands. I do all the repair jobs around here, even electric and plumbing repairs, and I build furniture. I keep thinking I got lost en route and totally missed my calling. My path? I'm getting so I mix my metaphors as badly as the kids I teach.'

Tate smiled. 'Sometimes I think I missed my calling, too. I've always suspected it was in the cards for me to have been an accountant.'

Bloch laughed and for a moment the two men looked at one another with the simplicity and directness of friends.

And me, Pedersen thought. If I'd studied psychology—he forced his mind back to the present moment. He had mulled enough in his lifetime over his helping to put people into cages as opposed to helping save them from themselves before they needed putting into cages. God, he thought, I'm like Ron with his wife. A Messiah complex. We all want someone to save.

* * *

Bloch led them back to the studio. Off the kitchen as it was, the workshop was far enough from the living-room so they could not, Pedersen noted, have been heard.

It was a small room lined with shelves and cupboards. Along the wall opposite the door, a

62

long pine worktable had been built under a wide window which looked directly into a lacework of roseate leaves. Heavenly bamboo. Pedersen thought of his own exuberant nandina bushes which needed pruning because he was never home long enough to clip them.

As the three men entered, two of the women he had met earlier turned from the table, on one end of which was set an impressive structure replicating a Victorian house of some substance. Alongside it was set another much smaller building done in the same style, which Pedersen recognized as a gazebo. Both appeared accurate as to scale; he could imagine a small figure in turn-of-the-century clothing standing at the door of the house with all else in perfect relationship. Pedersen thought, as he so often did: Now what would Freda think of all this?

Karin Bloch was not pleased to see him. 'Oh no—must you?' Seeing her this time, he realized she was a tall woman. With her tawny hair and her bearing, she brought to mind Vikings, princesses from northern regions. 'Does she *have* to answer more questions? I've just—we're just about to do some work. Dawn needs to get her mind off things for a little while.'

'It's all right.' Dawn's face was swollen and had lost its warm colour, but she seemed calm.

'Actually,' said Pedersen, 'I don't need to ask Miss Voletski anything more right now. I just asked your husband to let me look in on your workroom. I have a fondness for workrooms.'

Karin brightened. 'I—Dawn and I, she's helping—are working on a Victorian house, to scale, for the art museum. The September show. It's being used at the entrance, a tie-in with the show's theme.' She swung back the hinged front so he could see into the house.

Pedersen's admiration was real. 'Doesn't that work make you nervous? I could barely hold on to some of those tiny posts you've put in the—'

'Balustrade. No, I find it relaxes me. People react differently to this sort of work. Of course I can't do it for too long.'

'And you do this too?' Tate said to Dawn.

'Not the work. It does make me nervous. I've advised Karin a little. I studied architecture.' The face she turned to Tate was bleak. 'I think Karin has me working today as therapy.'

Karin was indignant. 'Working is always better than mulling, but you are helping. Really.' She addressed Tate. 'She's wonderful with all the little details—pediments and scrolled brackets and columns.'

'I can see why you need an architect,' Tate said.

'Perhaps,' said Pedersen to Karin, 'Mr Bloch could keep Dawn company for a few minutes and I could talk just with you?'

64

Keith Bloch picked up his cue. 'Come on, Dawn, I'll put you to work now. You can help me pick oranges for Marcie. I promised to take some up to her.' He led her out of the room.

Glancing at his partner's face, Pedersen said, 'Give them a hand, Ron. Tell him we'll carry the oranges up with us in a few minutes when we go to speak to Miss Terpstra.'

Alone with Karin, he said, 'This is a neighbourhood of artists and craftspeople, isn't it? You and your miniatures, Dawn with her pottery, Mr Follett and Miss Devane with their books. What else do we have here? Is Miss Terpstra an artist too? And Miss Morgan?'

'Marcie writes poetry, but I'm not sure she advertises the fact. Leona's with the art museum but only as a board member. There are others in the neighbourhood too.' She grinned. 'We're a bunch of people who like space to do things, that's why we live up here away from town. Until just lately it's been like living in the country. Not any more.' He thought of the new buildings going up.

'Your husband says your relationship with the neighbours is casual, yet a number of you celebrated Mr Follett's success with him. I gather some pretty personal exchanges took place at the party Miss Morgan gave.'

She looked blank.

'The business of someone's pushing Follett.'

'Oh, that. That was just Max. You had to know him to understand.'

'Just Max. That's a phrase I keep running across.'

'I'm not surprised. Max was like many artists, pretty self-involved. The world responded to him, rather than it's being the other way around, if you know what I mean. He was at the centre, the focus of everything that happened. It's a sort of arrogance that's shared by many creative people. They have to be focal—or feel they are. So if Max stumbled against a railing, he'd be sure it was no accident. Someone must have done it to him, pushed him, that would be his reasoning.'

'He sounds difficult. He had friends, though?'

'Of course. All of us, and many others. And women loved him. I suppose that was sex. He had a sort of appeal. He was big, handsome in a rugged way. It flattered them to think the Great Novelist was interested in them.' She looked at him. 'You think someone wanted him dead, don't you?'

'Did anyone?'

She bridled. 'What a question. How would I know, and if I did, would I say?'

He disarmed her with a smile. 'I'm sure not. May I drop by now and then to see how your creation is coming along?'

'Oh, come now, Detective, you know perfectly well that wouldn't be why you'd drop by. You don't have that much time.'

'No,' he said, 'I don't. But I expect to have to

be up here a few times until this matter is sorted out, and I do have a cabinetmaker's interest. I'm not flattering you.'

She looked unconvinced but pleased.

He glanced out of the window. 'I gather your relationship with Dawn is not as complicated as with her brother.'

'I wasn't aware I'd said it was complicated. But Dawn's great. She's been a good friend. So has Marcie. In fact all of us have good feelings about each other—maybe I misled you on that. It's just that we had to take Max as he was. Laugh him off when he was impossible. Even Dawn learned that. She's just out of a failed marriage and beginning to—' she smiled—'I guess the current phrase is "get her act together".'

'Not so current. I could give you a whole list of new phrases. Unfathomable.'

She laughed, a hearty, open-throated laugh. 'I have a couple of kids. I figure they'll tutor me as I go along.'

'They will, whether you like it or not.' He smiled. 'You and your husband have saved me a lot of busywork, Mrs Bloch.'

'Call me Karin.' She ran her fingers through her rough hair. It was the colour of the pine table. 'And come see my Victorian any time, Detective.' She stood facing him, feet solidly planted, head up, eyes on his, a Viking princess in complete possession of herself.

The orange pickers stood together, a loaded

67

basket next to them.

'We'll take it up,' said Pedersen. He looked at the mound of oranges. 'She'll have a time doing away with this.'

Keith shook his head. 'No trouble at all. Kevin's day care centre is having a party. She's the mother with the juice.' He laughed. 'I could have worded that better. Which reminds me. I have to get back to those papers.'

* * *

'Quite a woman, Karin Bloch,' Pedersen remarked as they carried the basket of oranges back to Marcie Terpstra's garage apartment. 'Tall.' He himself was drawn to small women.

'Very tall.'

'Impressive.'

'Very impressive.'

Pedersen looked at Tate and grinned. 'I liked her,' he said.

A slender bare-legged young woman, obviously brassiere-less under the clinging T-shirt, answered Pedersen's knock. The pattern on the full calf-length skirt was slightly a-tilt, giving it a homemade look that was not unappealing. She wore sandals. In the face under the chopped-off copper hair the teenager was not quite gone, but the smudges of purple beneath the eyes suggested the woman as well. She looked tired.

Marcie Terpstra's son was nowhere to be

seen, but a framed photograph on a bookcase showed him to be an imp-faced toddler with a froth of curly hair. Tate stopped to admire the picture, while the boy's mother relieved the older detective of the basket of fruit as though policemen daily dropped in delivering oranges.

'I heard you were paying visits in the neighbourhood,' she said. 'I saw the car in the drive, so I tucked Kevin in for his nap. He's a good little kid but he can be a distraction. To put it generously.' She smiled.

The apartment was barely adequate to house two. In the living-room a box springs and mattress had been pushed into a corner and covered with a cloth that looked as though the designer had scribbled on it with coloured crayon. Pedersen liked it. In the kitchen to which she led them a blue-painted table and matching chairs had been placed next to a window, with a high chair nearby. She had set out pottery mugs.

'Well. This is thoughtful,' said Tate.

'A little self-interest involved. If we talk in the living-room we may wake Kevin. He's been asleep awhile.' She poured steaming coffee into the mugs. 'How about a cookie? Homemade.'

'Why not?' said Pedersen. 'I've never said no to a homemade cookie in my life.'

She smiled, and her face altered, became impish. Like Freda, only with Freda it was the laugh that came in a surprised little explosion, as though she were startled and delighted by

69

her companion's wit. She hadn't been laughing much in the last few days.

'What I should do is ask you for the recipe for your cookies,' Pedersen said as he started on his third, 'but I'm afraid instead I'm going to have to ask you to tell me what you know about Max Follett.'

She stirred in her chair. 'Really, Detective, I don't think I can add anything. I knew him as a neighbour and a teacher. He teaches—taught a course each quarter in fiction-writing. I took it when I first came to Bay Cove. He was terribly demanding and ... critical. Unbelievably critical. By the time he was done with me— with most of us—we were sure we were just wasting our time. I dropped out finally and I haven't attempted any writing since.'

'But I understood you wrote poetry,' said Pedersen.

She looked annoyed. 'I don't know who told you that. I meant I haven't written any fiction since I took Max's class.'

'Was he interested in you—romantically?' Pedersen asked.

She shook her head vigorously. 'No. Somebody told you that too, I suppose. He liked me and he flirted with every woman he saw. It was Leona he was involved with.'

Pedersen nodded. 'Let me ask something less personal. You've been in the neighbourhood for a couple of years. Have you a sense that there was enmity between Mr

Follett and any of his neighbours?'

She looked puzzled. 'Oh. You're talking about his accident Saturday. His saying he was pushed? That was just Max.'

'That's a popular phrase regarding Mr Follett,' Tate remarked.

'It is?' She turned the full force of her smile on him. 'I'm not surprised.'

'So your own relationship with Mr Follett was slight. All the same, you must have—'

'No!' she interrupted with force. 'No, you don't. I'm not about to gossip about my neighbours. Any feelings they had, *they* can tell you.' Her lips folded in a firm line.

Pedersen was startled.

Tate spoke into the silence. 'You're divorced—a single mother?'

'We just lived together. When he found out I was pregnant, he took off.' She raised one hand and flicked her fingers. 'Evaporated.' No regrets, her voice said.

Pedersen cast a glance at the half-empty cookie plate and got up from his chair. 'We won't take up any more time, Miss Terpstra. If we think of anything else, we'll be in touch.'

'Yes,' said Tate. 'Thank you for the coffee. If we've forgotten something and have to come back, do we get more cookies?'

He wants her to smile too, thought Pedersen.

'I'm sorry Max is dead,' she said as she walked to the door with them. 'He could be difficult at times, but you don't want people to

71

die for that sort of thing.'

'Not usually.' Pedersen turned back at the door. 'But if it occurs to you that there *was* anyone who might have wanted him to die, for whatever reason, I hope you'll give us a call. Even if it's a neighbour.' He handed her a card. She accepted it, her face expressionless.

'I don't know how these single mothers do it,' Tate said as they walked around the garage and along the little concrete path. 'Imagine bringing up a kid on the pittance she must earn from that part-time job.'

But Pedersen didn't reply. He was busy with his own thoughts.

*   *   *

In the garage apartment, Marcie Terpstra was telephoning.

'Perry, this is Marcie. Sorry to break in on your work, but I want to ask something of you. Please don't discuss with the police what I told you Saturday.'

'You mean about Max's being after you?'

'Don't mention that, either. But I meant the other. You haven't mentioned it?'

'Of course not. I won't say anything. Although...'

'No, Perry. Just don't mention it. Oh damn, I hear Kevin waking up. I'll let you get back to your writing.'

She hung up and walked to the window. The

detectives were getting into their car. 'Coming, Kevin,' she called.

CHAPTER NINE

'I wonder why people make miniatures,' said Pedersen. They were walking slowly down the main road looking for access to the short cut that wound past the Follett property. They headed down the hill in the direction of Dawn's studio and, beyond, of town.

'Let me guess,' said Tate. 'They're childlike. Or they're threatened by big things. Or haven't the confidence to build on a large scale. Or maybe it gives them a sense of mastery— complete control over a perfect little world they've created. Am I getting warm?'

Pedersen let out a snort of laughter. 'I haven't the faintest idea. But join the Order of Armchair Psychologists— you're doing fine.'

'There's something intriguing, though, about building on such a small scale. You can grasp it. Ordinarily all sorts of things get in the way—your height relative to it, the buildings next to it, people going in and out, even the traffic. A miniature shows you the whole at a glance.'

'I wish something would show us the whole of this Follett business at a glance. Wait. I think this is our path.'

Weeds and shrubs had encroached to the

73

point where it was barely visible, a little footpath to their left. 'Only someone who knows the neighbourhood would ever be aware of this.' Pedersen craned to see whether it led where they thought. 'Shall we?'

Concealed by eucalyptus and the low growth that bordered the main road, the path twisted back up the hill into an open area. As they reached the top, across the wide space the two men could see the rear yard of the Devane house and, beyond, that of the Follett house.

'We're not visible from the main road,' said Tate.

'No. And if we cut off along the edge of this field I think we could make it to the side door of the Follett house without being seen by Devane.'

'Yes, that hedge cuts off most of her view.'

'Of course a jogger might have gone by on Follett's street at that hour.'

'They're usually in a trance.'

They walked past the Follett house, emerged on the little side road and headed around the corner to the main one and their car. On the Bloch property, no one was to be seen.

They drove slowly down the hill, rechecking the visibility of the path. 'Nice flowers,' Tate remarked, glancing across from the path to the other side of the road. 'What are they? Irises?'

Pedersen slowed further. 'They're like Florence Smith's. I wonder if they picked them here.' He glanced back across the road to the

74

path, and pulled the car to a stop. 'Irises like that don't grow wild, do they? I thought only blue flags did. I'm going to pick some, Freda's crazy about that bronze colour. I'll drop them off home, maybe they'll cheer her up.' He dug his Swiss army knife out of the glove compartment. 'Come on.'

Back in the car, Pedersen laughed. 'Do you realize what we could have done to the image of the Bay Cove cop if anyone had seen us? The *Banner* would have done a spread on it. *Soft Side of a Tough Guy*, they'd call it.'

'They'd be asking us if we eat quiche.' Tate glanced behind him. 'You don't think anyone did see us?'

'No, that little patch of road is concealed. You aren't really worried about it, are you, Ron?'

'No. It's just that I'm already regarded as odd enough with my wire-rimmed glasses and my interest in books. I don't want to confirm anyone's impression that I'm not the type for the police force, especially since I have my own doubts now and then.'

'Listen, it's different now, but when I came on the force no one with a college degree was trusted, no matter what eyeglasses he wore. We were bleeding hearts—no street savvy, the guys thought. There's still some of that, of course. The town was smaller then. They gave us a map and a penal code and the keys to a patrol car and we were in business. For that, who needed

75

an education? There wasn't even a police academy, let alone men who could waive the requirement because they were already educated.'

'That was all before the university came in?'

'Yes. The university did change things. Freda says it's all for the good, but when you think that women are afraid to walk downtown late at night now, I wonder. Attracting people to a university doesn't mean attracting just campus types. When a city grows, it grows in all directions.' He turned right, towards the heart of town. 'Well. We should be mapping out some sort of strategy where this case is concerned.'

'We're treating it as murder, right?'

'It sure as hell wasn't an accident. Suicide, maybe, but the evidence says no.' They pulled into the headquarters parking lot.

Tate unbuckled his seat-belt, his face clouded with doubt. 'That's the likeliest bunch of murder suspects I've ever seen.'

'You know how much that means.' Pedersen glanced at his partner. 'You liked Marcie Terpstra, didn't you?'

Tate looked surprised. 'Terpstra? Oh, she had a cute grin. Actually I kind of...' He looked self-conscious. 'I felt sorry for the sister. Voletski. Dawn. Poor kid.'

Pedersen laughed.

'What's so funny?'

'Oh, nothing, a thought that went through

my head. Just remember, Terpstra or Voletski, keep your objectivity. Till the case is closed, at least.'

Tate's face had grown pink. 'Naturally.' He looked offended.

'I just don't want you convincing any of our colleagues that men in wire-rimmed glasses don't have their minds on their work.' Pedersen grinned as they entered the building.

*   *   *

Carl Pedersen hated paperwork. Like most of his breed, he was a detective who preferred work in the field to work at the desk. He had continued on as a detective-sergeant although his eligibility to compete for the rank of lieutenant, with consequent administrative responsibility, had been established; periodically he reminded himself that all he had to do was take the test. But only after the introduction of longevity pay had he continued comfortably in his present job. Now that the Powers-That-Be had seen the wisdom of keeping crack detective-sergeants in the field, he, a proven senior officer, could do what he did best without guilt over his family.

Ronald Tate was the ideal partner for him, the perfect complement. Tate thrived on detail, he had youth and education and he was assertive without being aggressive. Pedersen's suggestions and instructions magically translated themselves into neatly stacked folders of information and hard evidence. It was comforting to Pedersen to think of what he didn't have to do because of Ron Tate.

'All right,' Pedersen said, as they reached his office. 'Let's see what's what.'

Tate flipped open his notebook. 'The PM. Background checks. Prints. The university. His publisher.'

'And a statement from Perry Devane. Oh, and keys.'

'Keys? You mean to Follett's house?'

'Yes. Dawn Voletski thought she had one someplace, she thought in a bowl on the bookshelf, but while I was there, she checked. Couldn't find it.'

'Did she think it might have been picked up by someone?'

'I asked that. She said she just wasn't too careful about keeping track of things.' Pedersen smiled. 'Like me.'

'But there's a possibility someone's lifted it.'

'Yes. We should check who runs in and out of her apartment, who might have had access to the key. Maybe after you get some of the paperwork done, you can take her on.'

Tate closed his notebook. 'That should keep me busy for a half-hour or so.'

'At least.' Pedersen was suddenly tired. 'Don't try to do it all at once. It'll still be there tomorrow.' He stood up heavily. 'I need some coffee. Oh. The irises.'

*　　*　　*

Walking back to his car, his spirits lightened. He'd drop off the flowers, have a quick cup of coffee with Freda, see if he could smooth things out a bit between them. Arthur Smith would simply have to wait an hour for the pleasure of his company.

*　　*　　*

Freda accepted the bronze irises without comment and laid them on the kitchen table at which she was sitting. He bent to kiss her. She turned her head. This distance, the sullenness, was so unlike her that he experienced an unfamiliar hollowness in his belly.

'Freda, has something new happened?'

'Not really.' After a minute she added, 'Just another letter from Clara.' She extracted it from the pocket of her denim skirt. It had been folded and refolded many times.

He took it from her and read it. It was a bitter letter. 'Sweetie, your sister's having a hard time with your mother. You know that.'

'Go ahead, side with her.' She swung around. 'Don't you even see what she's saying? All you have to do is read between the lines. She wishes Mother were dead. *Dead!*'

'Freda!' He was shocked.

'She does. She sounds as though Mother is

79

something used up, irrelevant. Just a nuisance, in everyone's way.'

He had never seen her like this. He became suddenly aware of how tired he was. 'Give me something to put the flowers into.'

She shook her head. 'You needn't. I'll do it.' She carried the blossoms to the sink and reached for a grey glass bowl. 'I'm sorry,' she said unrepentantly. 'You just don't understand. *Your* mother's fine.'

After a while he said, 'You heard about Max Follett?'

'Yes. What was it? An accident?'

'I doubt it.'

'Murder?' She turned to him, the bowl of flowers in her hand. 'He got in somebody's way, too? He made somebody's life difficult?'

* * *

Later, driving to the Greengrove Nursery, he reflected on the conversation. It was not like Freda, so naturally ebullient, to be so negative, so depressed. So angry. Especially so angry with him.

He thought back to her last words. *Had* Max Follett got in someone's way? Made life unbearable for someone? It was hardly a comparable situation, but he supposed there were parallel features. He sighed. He wished the day were over and he were in bed.

The Greengrove Nursery was made up of

two long low buildings between which could be glimpsed greenhouses to the rear. One building appeared to be devoted to the sale of insecticides, fertilizers, other garden preparations and ceramic containers for potting and garden tools. At one end was an open door above which hung a sign identifying it as the office. Through the open door Pedersen could see a man seated at a desk studying a scrap of paper.

He approached the door. 'Mr Smith?'

A thin, balding man with a gentle face looked up and smiled. 'Yes. Can we do something for you? I think there's someone...' He peered past Pedersen towards several clerks who moved among the customers.

'No,' Pedersen broke in. 'It's you I want to see, Mr Smith.' He took out his identification. 'Detective Pedersen.'

'Oh.' The man's face changed. 'Sit down. It's Max, I suppose.'

'Yes. If you have a minute.'

Arthur Smith laughed shortly. 'Oh, I have one. I was just trying to decipher this.' He thrust the half-sheet of paper at Pedersen, reading aloud as he did so:

1. That rock rose with the little red flower, the one I told you I saw in that garden in Lewistown.
2. The thing I thought was buckwheat. It begins with P.

3. That stuff my gardener calls society
   garlic. It has little lilac blossoms on tall
   stems. Very splashy.

'Would you think,' he finished, 'that Mrs
Williams is one of Bay Cove's finest gardeners?
She knows just what she wants, she just doesn't
know what anything is called.'

Pedersen asked with real curiosity, 'What
will you send her?'

'Oh, the first is *Helianthemum nummularium*
and the lilac flower would be *Allium giganteum*,
but who knows which of the *Polygonums* she
wants? But you didn't come to talk about
horticulture.'

'No. Although I admired your taste in irises
so much I picked some for my wife.'

Arthur Smith looked up quickly. 'Irises.
Oh.' His face closed as though he had drawn a
curtain across it. 'You've been to my house.'

'Yes. Mrs Smith was very forthcoming. I
gather from her, and from several others, that
Max Follett was not a man likely to win any
popularity prizes.'

'No. Of course since my wife was at one time
married to him, I'm inclined to be biased.' His
manner remained distant. 'What did you want
to ask me?'

Pedersen, playing it by ear, decided
instantly. 'I wondered what you thought about
Mr Follett's near-fatal accident Saturday
evening.' Smith looked blank. 'At the party for

him.'

'Oh.' He paused as though deciding what to answer. 'He bumped against the rotten fence railing.'

'Hadn't you all been warned about that?'

'Leona thought there was some sort of termite damage. I don't think we took it very seriously.'

'Could someone have pushed Mr Follett? Accidentally or on purpose?'

'Either is possible. It's also possible he was just careless.'

'Did you yourself see him close to the railing?'

In an abrupt burst of impatience Arthur Smith said, 'He caught hold of me to save himself, but what difference does all this make? The man's dead. And not from falling in a ravine.' Under the thinning hair, the narrow face was flushed.

Pedersen took another tack. 'Did you find Max Follett paranoid, suspicious without real basis for suspicion?'

'You know—' Smith enunciated his words with care—'I can only say one thing about Max Follett with real authority. That is that I avoided him whenever possible.'

'It must have been a bit difficult, with his living right around the corner. Could I ask, did your wife continue to be friendly towards him?'

Smith laughed, a tart, bitter sound. 'We all went through the motions of being friendly.

Florence still felt some—concern for him, they were married for years. I found him hard to take, but I never made an issue of it.'

'I see. Had either of you spoken to him recently?'

A shadow passed across Smith's face. 'We saw him Saturday.'

'I meant aside from the party.'

The ready answer surprised Pedersen. 'He came by Saturday afternoon.'

'To buy plants?'

'Follett? He had no interest in plants. He just came to talk. To needle me in his subtle fashion.' There was pain in the man's face. 'He'd just had a cup of coffee with my wife.'

Pedersen found it hard to hold his ground, his empathy with the man was so strong. 'Despite his—needling, you went to the party for him?'

'I told you, I never made an issue of my feelings. I was the only one of his neighbours who felt as I did about him, I wasn't going to flaunt my—'

'Jealousy?'

'Jealousy? It wasn't jealousy.' His eyes were cold.

'Was there something in particular he came to needle you about?'

Smith stood up so suddenly his chair tilted precariously and Mrs William's list fluttered to the ground. He was a tall man. 'Nothing I care to discuss, Detective.' It was a dismissal.

84

On his way out of the Greengrove, Pedersen paused beside a white azalea in a tub. Freda would like that. He checked himself. This wasn't the time. He continued on his way.

TUESDAY

CHAPTER TEN

Karin woke late, her body aching as though she had been pounded all over. Beside her Keith lay sprawled on his side of the bed, looking as though he might never move again. The clock confirmed what the light had already told her. Almost eight. She had forgotten to set the alarm.

'Keith! Keith! It's late.' She shook him with all the vigour she could muster.

He moaned and rolled over, opening his eyes long enough to take in the clock. 'Five minutes.'

'Five. I'll get the kids up. *Five*, really, Keith.'

In the kitchen she plugged in the coffee-pot and switched on the radio. A dispirited young woman was announcing morning ragas on the university station; she flicked it off again.

As though they too were emotionally exhausted, the children were intolerably slow. By the time she had prodded them through their oatmeal, Karin found herself barely able to contain her irritation. Keith was no more patient. When at last he crossly nudged the children into the car and pulled out of the drive, she sighed with relief and poured herself a second cup of coffee.

Sitting over the steaming cup, sifting through the events of the previous day, she gradually felt the ache in her lower back ease. She drifted into drowsy contemplation of the bar of sunlight that lay across her hands. Capable, she thought, that's what they call hands like mine. They can do anything I want them to do. In a way it was good that Dawn had not been persuaded to stay overnight. Suddenly she was eager to get back to work.

Leaving the dishes soaking in the sink, she opened the door to her studio. What she saw took a moment to register. The Victorian structure stood in the sunlight that lay on the table, compactly elegant, awaiting further work; but alongside it the diminutive gazebo lay smashed, splintered as though someone had dealt it a crushing blow with a hammer. She stood with her hand over her mouth, incredulous, barely breathing.

Nothing else was disturbed. Tools hung neatly on the pegboard, the little stacks of wood were not an inch out of place, the house plan tacked to the wall lay flat and smooth.

She spoke aloud. 'How...' and heard her own voice in the empty room. Backing out of the studio as though it still held the vandal, she made for the kitchen telephone extension.

*   *   *

In his office Pedersen's phone rang.

'Detective Pedersen?'

'Yes,' he repeated, 'this is Detective Pedersen.' He thought he recognized the frightened voice. 'Mrs Bloch? Is something the matter?'

'Yes, we've had a break-in. Could you come?'

'I'll send—'

'No, you come. I have a feeling it has something to do with what happened yesterday.'

'I see. I'll be there in ten minutes. Are you in the house?'

'Yes.' Her voice quavered. *I'm* all right. There's no one here now. Just come.'

*   *   *

She was waiting for him. 'Somebody got in.' Her face was white.

She led him through the kitchen. Around him he saw no particular disorder, no piece of furniture overturned, nothing broken.

'It's in the studio,' she explained, her voice uneven. 'Before we went to bed last night I turned out the light in there. Everything was fine then. But this morning—look!' She flung open the door.

87

Pedersen bent to look more closely at the debris of the tiny summerhouse.

'I don't see why,' Karin wailed. 'Why would someone ruin my work this way? What's *happening* in this neighbourhood, anyway?' He could hear that she was struggling not to cry. 'It was so little, it took days and days to build,' she cried, her voice departing.

He looked around. 'Any tools missing? Hammers?'

She calmed somewhat as her eyes ran over the pegboard. 'I don't think so. Everything's in place—I always put my tools away.'

'How about the kids?' At her expression, he went on, 'Kids do unpredictable things, sometimes for reasons we can't understand. Could it have been one of them?'

Karin crossed her arms over her chest and tipped her chin back. 'Never. Surely you can do better than that, Detective.'

'Who was in the house? Who has access to it?'

'No one. Just my family. Keith and I don't always lock doors, but we did last night, after...'

Pedersen leaned across the table. Without touching it, he examined the open window above the table. 'You left this open?'

She shook her head, then nodded. 'I may have. It was open yesterday. But the screen was in.'

It was no longer in.

88

The window opened on to a wide strip between their yard and the Smiths'. Outside beneath the window they found the screen. Stepping carefully and using the tips of his fingers, Pedersen eased the window down. It slid smoothly, noiselessly. 'You keep your house in good repair,' he remarked. 'If it was opened in the night, you'd never have heard it.'

'That's Keith. He fixed it, it used to stick.' She stood close to him between the clump of nandina and the house and reached past him to point. Splinters lay on the ground; the earth was scuffed.

'Yes. There are bits of earth among the broken pieces on your worktable. And the pieces are all heaped together.'

'That's how they did it? Broke it up out here? That must be why we didn't hear anything. We sleep on the other side of the house.'

'I'll check for fingerprints on the screen, but I doubt we'll find much.' He shook his head. 'Fingerprints are highly overrated when it comes to solving most crimes.'

They made their way back to the house, Karin Bloch oddly deflated, as though some essential stiffening of her tall frame had failed and she had shrunk.

'Do you think somebody's out to get us? All of us?' she said.

'Maybe not all. Think now. What motive could anyone have for destroying your work?'

'I can't imagine. It can't be jealousy, I don't

know another soul who's doing just what I am. Dawn's going to feel awful. The gazebo was her idea.'

'Did anyone know that?'

'Know it was her idea? I should think everyone, it was in the *Banner*.' She indicated a newspaper article pinned to her bulletin board. 'They did this article on the Victorian house, used both our photographs, Dawn with the gazebo, me with the house. Everybody saw it. They were even talking about it at Max's party.'

Pedersen stood reading the article. 'Was this just one of many ideas of hers or the only one?'

'One of several, but the gazebo was the only one publicized, and it was special for her. Her family had one when she was a kid. Her parents built it for her as a playhouse. She's going to be really upset about this.'

Pedersen was silent, watching her face as she stood thinking.

'Detective,' she said suddenly, 'could it be— not me, but—' Her face was a question.

'But?'

'Dawn. Could it have been Dawn they were trying to hurt?'

'Follett's sister.'

Blankly, she returned his gaze. 'Max—and now Max's sister. *Why?*'

CHAPTER ELEVEN

Dawn was in her garden picking chives from a large clay pot, her face crinkled with concentration. She jumped when Tate spoke.

'Hi. Am I interrupting?'

She looked confused. 'Interrupting? Oh, this.'

'Can you spare a few minutes?' He looked at her face more closely. Beneath the mop of dark curls, it was pale. 'Are you up to it?'

'Yes, but can we go in? I have to put these in the refrigerator.'

Inside, Tate noted that she had been working at her pottery; an oddly-shaped piece that looked like—what? a vegetable? a crookneck squash, he decided—sat on her worktable as though she had just stepped out of the room a minute and planned to return. She laid the handful of chives on a bookcase and wandered over to the table to lay a damp cloth over her work.

'The refrigerator?' Tate said.

She looked at him vaguely and then remembered. As she put the chives away, he thought: Well, work is a good sign. 'Are you feeling any better today?' he asked.

'Some. I'm trying to do things. I can't not do anything, I just cry. I called the funeral home—chapel, they call it. Max would hate that. He

91

was an atheist. Vehement. He wanted cremation. The ... body will be released today and the chapel said they would be able to ...' She left the last sentence unfinished. 'I'll have to think what to do about a memorial service.'

'Someone got through to his publisher, I see.'

'Yes, we called yesterday. Did they say something on the radio this morning?'

'TV.'

She indicated a chair and sat down uncertainly opposite him. 'What do you need me to tell you?' She crossed her legs. She wore the denim skirt; today's hose and shirt were pink. He liked the tidiness of her work outfit.

Taking out his notebook, he said, 'I need some idea of the people who might have picked up that key to your brother's house. Detective Pedersen says you usually keep it in a bowl in this room.'

'I do. I haven't really searched for it, though, maybe it's in a pocket or something. You think someone *stole* it?'

'We're wondering. Miss Voletski—'

'Dawn.'

'Dawn, have you talked with Karin Bloch this morning?'

'No. Should I have?'

'You haven't heard about the gazebo?'

'No. The gazebo?'

'During the night someone demolished it— hammered or stomped it to splinters.'

Incredulity touched her face. 'Demolished it?'

'Completely.' He removed his glasses, polished them, put them back. 'The gazebo was your idea, wasn't it?'

'Yes, but—'

'Does that suggest anything to you?'

'No. Oh dear, the gazebo.' She pulled her attention back to him. 'What should it suggest?'

'We're a little concerned that it may not just be your brother who is the target.'

'You mean *me*? You think that's what it means?'

'We don't know. Nothing else in the studio was touched.'

She considered the idea for a few moments. Then she said, her voice bitter, 'Good thing there aren't any more of us Folletts.'

He ignored that. 'We're concerned about protecting you. If your brother was murdered, the sooner we find the person responsible the safer you'll be. You see why I'm interested in that key.'

'Did the—person have a key to the Blochs' house, too?'

'No, that was done differently. Now, what about the key?'

She got up slowly as though moving were an effort. 'First let me look for it. Do you want me to do it now?'

'If you would. I have the time.'

The apartment was small but not untidy. He watched as she went through the clothes closet. Jeans and skirts made up most of her wardrobe. After she had checked jeans pockets, dug her hand into a bathrobe pocket, overturned her handbag, checked skirts and jackets, she closed the closet and began on the room. No bowl or tray or drawer or bookshelf yielded up the key.

Tate watched her as she searched. She moved neatly, efficiently. He was unsure what had made her so appealing to him, what about the small sturdy figure and earnest face roused this tenderness in him that made it hard to maintain an appropriate reserve.

Finally she spread both hands in a gesture of defeat. 'Dumb. I should have a regular place for things like keys.' She rechecked the small bowl on her worktable. 'Usually it's here. Well, I can't seem to find it.' She sat down again. 'I don't see—you want the names of the people who visit me? They'd never take it. What will you do with the names?'

He smiled. 'One thing I promise we won't do is rush your friends down to headquarters and submit them to the third degree.'

Unexpectedly she gave a little laugh. Tate's heart expanded.

'Look,' she said, getting up, 'would you like some herb tea while we talk? I have Orange Spice and Sleepytime.'

'What is Sleepytime?'

94

'Just a name. I'll make you some.' Her mood had lightened.

'All right,' she said after she had filled their cups. 'I don't have that many visitors and I know none of them would have taken the key, but I'll tell you. I did see that key last week, I'm sure, so why don't I tell you everyone I can think of since then?'

He pulled his pen from his pocket.

'There are the Blochs, at least Karin. I can't remember if Keith—yes, he brought me down some tomatoes. And Florence came by one morning. Perry, let me think. I guess so. Not Arthur. Marcie's in and out all the time. Leona, no. That's all the people from around here I ever see. Those are the ones you're interested in, aren't they? Any other friends of mine wouldn't know Max. Not,' she added, 'that I have all that many friends. I've sort of kept to myself—' she smiled faintly—'licking my wounds, I suppose. I was divorced recently. To my brother's delight.'

'Me, too. I mean I'm divorced too,' Tate said, warm with fellow feeling. 'It's hard.'

'You get addicted to people, don't you?' she said solemnly.

He laughed. 'I never thought of it that way. Maybe addicted to being married. How long did yours last?'

'Almost five years. My brother had his doubts it'd last five months.'

'Mine was four years. I guess I'm still not

95

really over it.'

'Did you run?'

'Run? You mean jog?'

'No—*run*. Keep going all the time—busy busy busy? I think to keep from facing it.'

'A kind of denial. I guess I did. I know I seemed to do nothing but work, afterwards. I'd wonder where the week had gone and every night I'd fall into bed, exhausted.'

'Just as well.' They stared at each other, separately contemplating the unpartnered bed, the single setting at the table.

'Had you always lived alone before?'

She squinted at him. 'Is this a police question or a personal one?'

'Personal.' And I'd better cut it out, he thought, but he waited for her reply.

'Well, of course when I was a kid I lived at home. Max was there till I was five or six and after that it was just me and my parents. I was born late. I guess my mother thought she'd finished having children, she'd had trouble having even the first.' She stopped, then she went on. 'My folks overprotected me, fussed over me.'

'The gazebo?'

'Yes, they had it built specially for me as a playhouse. They'd built a treehouse for Max when he was little.' Her eyes filled. 'I miss him. Funny, in some ways he was terrible to me, but I adored him. I never understood him, but I know he loved me.'

'He sounds like a rather complicated man. He probably took his troubles out on you, since you were so close to him.'

'Maybe.' She mopped at her eyes with her forefinger.

'I know it's hard for you to talk about.'

'It's all right. Maybe it's even better. While I was in high school, my father died. Then, as soon as I was old enough to get out from under my mother's coddling, I went to another city to live.' She sighed. 'But she wasn't well, she died not long after that. So, to answer your question—at length—' she gave a wry little smile—'I've been on my own for quite a while. I've depended on Max a lot, though. For better or for worse.'

'He was a sort of parent?'

'A demanding one.' Her eyes had dried. 'I'd have done better to have moved somewhere further from Max, but when Will and I split up, I just reached out. Max was all I had.' She looked across at him. 'It was strange. The whole thing was strange.'

'Family relationships are. We all have ... ambivalent feelings about our families. We need them and want them and, I don't know, want them to let go, all at the same time.'

'And your marriage?'

'It was a first marriage. We spent our whole time getting it together, and then we split.'

'People are crazy. Seems to me I've spent all my life getting it together, discovering who I

97

am and what I want. I'm doing better, though. Or I was.'

'Seems to me you're doing just fine.'

'Working in a health food store part time?' She raised her eyebrows. Some of the rosy colour had returned to her face. 'But I've found something I love—the pottery. Max thought it was trivial, but he even felt that way when I studied architecture. I never understood why he was that way about anything I did. It was never right. You know what I mean?'

'He was probably a perfectionist—for you both.' Something in him tugged; he wanted to cross the room to her, cup the solemn face, look into the dark eyes, pull her to him. He stood abruptly and said, his voice overloud, 'I'd better be on my way.'

She looked surprised. 'Well, yes. Did you like the Sleepytime?'

He looked down into his empty cup. He had not tasted it. 'Yes, good,' he said. 'Very good. Wonderful.'

She followed him, her face puzzled, and let him out.

'If I think of any more people, I'll call you,' she said. Then: 'Where—?'

He gave her his card. 'I'm sorry about the gazebo. You watch yourself.' He wasn't sure how she could do that. 'Be careful. Lock doors.'

She nodded. 'I will.'

Tate shook his head as he walked down the

path and pushed the stubborn gate open. Maybe in the future someone else should handle the interviews with Dawn Voletski.

* * *

The post-mortem revealed nothing they might not have expected. The reconstruction of events appeared accurate; however, one feature of the affair came as a surprise: the technician had discovered the hair-drier was not only old, it was defective.

The technician shook his head. 'It must have been dropped, probably on that hard bathroom tile. The wonder is the guy didn't electrocute himself long ago.' When he was reached, the manufacturer's representative explained to Tate at great length that even the older models were insulated, if perhaps not quite so thoroughly as the newer ones. The representative's voice became slightly querulous as he continued. '*Naturally*,' he said, aggrieved at the public and its deplorable behaviour, 'we expect that the appliance will be handled with care and not dropped or struck against hard surfaces. No electrical appliance will stand up to *that* sort of thing. Or to being used around water. There are warnings right on the driers.' He was clearly envisioning a legal suit that, considering the public relations quotient of Max Follett, could be devastating.

'Doesn't tell us much, all that,' said Tate

after he had recounted the conversation to Pedersen. 'Who could know the hair-drier had been damaged?'

'No one. People just assume that electrical appliances in water are lethal, they've been warned so many times. Don't you assume that?'

'Well, I wouldn't experiment to find out if it's true.'

'Exactly.'

'So the person who dropped that drier just got lucky?'

Pedersen frowned. 'You could put it like that.'

Accident appeared out of the question. With the gazebo incident, suicide seemed more far-fetched than before, and since the assault on the miniature, Pedersen's sense of urgency had increased.

'What,' he said, '*don't* we know that brought someone's wrath down on both of them?'

'Something earlier?' Tate asked. 'Something someone knows about their past life? Or someone who knew them before, how about that?'

'Maybe. Of course it may be something right here and now.' Pedersen reached into his desk for a packet of peanuts. He had given up offering them to Tate. 'With Follett,' he said, 'it should be easy. His life has been examined. We can probably find out pretty much everything from Day One without trouble. The sister is another matter, and apparently she has no idea herself why she'd be a target.'

'Maybe simply because she's his sister.'

Pedersen removed another peanut from the packet and broke it in half, checking for the dwarf in the centre as he and his father had done when he was a boy. 'Maybe,' he said dubiously. 'Dawn was married. Her husband might know something. We should look him up.'

'And look into his motives, his relationship with them. Follett opposed the marriage. There must have been no love lost between them.' Tate paused. 'About Dawn.' He stopped.

'Yes?'

'Maybe—oh, nothing.'

Pedersen studied his face. 'Worried about talking with her so much while she's still upset over her brother? We have to, Ron. We don't want any more accidental electrocutions.'

'I know. It's just—' He seemed to be in some sort of struggle with himself.

'OK, then?' Pedersen looked at him for a minute and gave up. From his desk he picked up the little wire string with green beads and dropped them in the pocket that held no peanuts. 'Freda,' he remarked without humour, 'is still mad at me.'

'Oh.'

'She thinks I'm too preoccupied with work. Not paying attention to her problems.'

'A policeman's lot.'

'No. She's not like that, not usually.'

'She liked the flowers?'

'As much as she noticed them. Later on she said they were pretty but had nothing to do with the matter at hand.' He sighed.

'Women,' said Tate. It was almost a question.

CHAPTER TWELVE

Pedersen and Tate found Dawn presiding over the counter of Hardin's Health Foods, surrounded by shelves of bottles and tins with scientific-looking labels in orange and black. She was explaining slowly and in some detail to an uncertain-looking middle-aged woman the virtues of a calcium-magnesium product.

Stacks of local give-away newspapers were piled on the floor; while they waited, Pedersen read an article on the mind's influence over gall-bladder function and looked up his horoscope in a journal dedicated primarily to astrology. The horoscope suggested that this was a fine time for him to involve himself in a new romance, and promised it would live up to his pleasurable expectations. The exhortation appeared to have overlooked some essential aspects of his character and the day ahead.

Tate stood to one side and watched Dawn. When the transaction was complete, he said,

'I'm studying your merchandising style. Soft sell, I'd say.'

She shrugged. 'I'm not convinced calcium preparations do a thing. What I'd like to sell that woman on is a long walk every day. Well, to what do I owe this visit?'

Pedersen put the newspaper down. 'I'm surprised you're back at work so soon.'

'There isn't anything else I can do. I can't go through my brother's papers yet and I can't—I decided I might as well be at work. They've been good to me here; I don't like to take their money and not work.'

Pedersen came to the point. 'Actually we aren't here to talk to you, Dawn. What we really need is your former husband's address.'

'Will's address? Why?' Her voice was cold. 'What can he possibly tell you? He barely knew Max, and he and I haven't had one thing to do with one another for over a year. I don't see any reason for your talking to him.'

Pedersen skirted a direct response. 'We need to talk to everybody connected with anyone in this affair, you must understand that.' He could see that she did not understand.

Uncharacteristically, Tate took over, more forthright. 'Look, Dawn, your former husband may still have strong feelings about the divorce. You were assaulted—indirectly, it's true, maybe only symbolically, but we should be sure just where he stands in relation to you and your family.'

'My *family*? My brother, you mean.' She looked at Tate thoughtfully. 'Will wasn't happy about the divorce, but he never in this world would—oh, all right, go talk to him.' She shrugged. 'See for yourselves.' His name was William Harner, she told them, he was a social worker with the Family Service Agency.

As they were on their way out, Pedersen turned back. 'Please don't alert him that we're coming.' She did not respond.

Walking along the outdoor mall from the health food store, Tate nodded as though Pedersen had spoken. 'Drop-in visit, that's best. He should be back from lunch.'

* * *

Will Harner had returned from lunch and had no appointment until three. He seemed unsurprised by the visit.

'Max Follett,' he announced, after they had seated themselves across the desk from him. He was a slight, sandy-haired man with a contemplative air about him. Not, Pedersen noted, the sort one would immediately fix on as a murderer. Harner smiled, something wry in his expression, as though he were reading Pedersen's thoughts.

'Yes, it is about Follett. Your former wife gave us your address.' Pedersen frowned. 'Not altogether willingly.'

Harner nodded. 'Doris and I haven't had

any contact recently. I suppose she wants to keep it that way.' His words were matter-of-fact. Pedersen wondered if the subject of Dawn truly evoked so little emotion.

'What,' he said, 'were your reactions when you read of your former brother-in-law's death?'

'If you want the truth—' Harner laughed shortly—'my first thought was that it could have been predicted. The bastard only got what was coming to him.' He smiled, as if he had made the blandest of statements.

'You disliked him?'

'Not enough to do him in.' Pedersen looked up sharply, and Harner responded to the glance. 'Yesterday's news-story suggested you think this wasn't a simple accident. Despite police disclaimers.'

'They weren't disclaimers, we're not sure yet what it was.' Pedersen leaned forward. 'Do you know of any particular enemies he had who perhaps did feel strongly enough to do him in?'

Harner shook his head. 'No. You have to realize I really didn't know the man well, even if he was my brother-in-law. And I didn't know any of his associates. Certainly not anyone who was—' he grimaced—'an *enemy.*'

'If you knew him so slightly,' Tate interjected, 'why do you refer to him as a bastard?'

Harner looked from one detective to another. 'Doris didn't tell you? He tried to break up our marriage. He didn't succeed, but he tried.'

Pedersen nodded. 'In what way did he try?'

Harner sat back. 'To begin with, he never approved of the marriage. Right at the outset Doris told me that.'

'You know,' Tate put in, 'she calls herself Dawn now.'

'I guess I did hear that. She was Doris when I was married to her. Anyway, Doris told me Max said it wouldn't last a year, I was a wimp. He saw all social workers as interfering do-gooders.' He smiled faintly. 'Not that there aren't some like that. Then when our marriage had lasted not only a year but two, then three, and finally five, I gather he gave up trying to smear me.'

'He had a lot of influence over Doris?' Pedersen asked.

'Doris isn't easily pushed around, but he was all the family she had and it was hard for her to keep her interests and opinions separate from his, at least while I knew her.'

'What finally did break you up?' Tate asked.

'To tell the truth, I don't think Doris fitted into our life any longer. She'd started taking ceramics classes. She'd overcome some of her shyness and was reaching out, making friends of her own. She wasn't any longer just my wife.'

Tate frowned. 'It would be odd these days for a woman without children to be ... just a wife.'

'It was odd. Actually it was I who tried to urge her to branch out. She was still a little girl in too many ways. Of course it didn't occur to me that my efforts would push her right out of our marriage. But, though I wasn't happy to lose her, I think she's better off now in most ways. She needs a time of being on her own.'

Pedersen grinned. 'Spoken like a true social worker.'

Harner looked doubtful. 'I've never felt like one, not with Doris.'

Pedersen sobered immediately. 'We have something else to ask you. Can you tell us anything about the Follett family? Anything in the past history of the family that could cause Max or Dawn—Doris—to be the subject of someone's anger? Or violence?'

Harner looked up sharply. 'Doris?'

'Would there have been resentment towards him—or her—*because* he was part of the Follett family?'

Harner raised his hands, palms up. 'Doris never mentioned anything, if there was anything to mention.' He came back to Pedersen's original question. 'Is someone after *Doris?*'

'We don't know. What about the parents?'

'Ordinary people, I gathered. The father sold medical supplies, the mother stayed home. They died fairly young. That left only Max and Doris. He must have taken her father's place in

107

a lot of ways, but like all fathers and father-surrogates, he didn't like to see his little girl grow up and get married.'

'Where did Doris grow up?' Pedersen asked.

'A little town four hours north of here. Longville. I've never been there. The parents were gone by the time I met Doris, and she and Max had already sold the house. I think she thinks of the place now and then. It always sounded very Middle America to me.'

'You're pretty understanding,' Tate said. 'I mean, considering that you didn't want out of the marriage.'

'Accepting is the word. For a long time the word was resigned. But it may all have been for the best, not only for Doris. I've met someone recently . . .' He let the sentence trail off.

Pedersen rose. 'Well, thanks for your help, Mr Harner.'

The anxiety Harner had expressed earlier resurfaced. 'Doris is all right, isn't she? No one's done anything to her?'

Pedersen avoided Tate's eyes. 'She's just fine. Hard at work dispensing health food.'

'Good.' Harner walked to the outer door with them. 'If you think of anything else I can do to help, let me know. Doris must be pretty broken up about this whole business. If you see her, tell her I'm sorry.'

'She is upset, but she's strong now, able to handle things. Just as you said.' Tate spoke with conviction.

Did Harner say that? Pedersen wondered. He glanced at Tate. Nothing in his co-worker's face told him anything.

*　　*　　*

'That didn't add up to much,' Tate said as they strolled towards the car. 'Nice guy, though.'

'He is. He seems to have recovered from the divorce. Already involved elsewhere.'

'I could take a page from his book.'

'Freda says you will when you're ready.'

'Readiness is all.' Tate sighed. 'Well, we'll see.' As they rounded the corner, Tate stiffened. 'Isn't that Mrs Bloch, loaded down with packages?'

'It is. Let's give her a hand.'

Karin Bloch turned to them with relief. 'Oh, wonderful. I'm going to drop this one for sure.' She put a huge, bulky package into Tate's arms.

'What *is* this?' he asked.

She laughed. 'It's a thirty-cup coffee-maker. I'm having a meeting at the house tonight and my old one has lost its handle. And most of its chrome, I might add.'

'What sort of meeting is that, Mrs Bloch?' Pedersen inquired. He had taken the smaller packages.

Her face clouded. 'A MADD meeting. Here's my car.' She unlocked her trunk and stowed the packages in it. 'Thanks a lot. You saved my life.' She was in the car and had pulled out before they could respond.

Pedersen and Tate looked at each other. 'MADD. Do you suppose she lost a kid to a drunk driver?' Tate said.

'I can't think why else she'd be having a meeting.' They continued to their car without speaking.

As Pedersen manoeuvred the car back into traffic, he said, 'What about the will? Anything on that yet?'

'Not yet. The lawyer said Follett never had him draw up a will, despite a warning that if he had any special bequests to make he'd better get to it. The last time he saw Follett, Follett said not to worry, he'd written one himself. So there must be a holograph will somewhere among those papers in his study.'

Pedersen shook his head. 'That means if we want to see it, we're going to have to go over there and really dig. God, I dread that job. By the way, what did the *Banner* say that gave Harner the notion Follett's death wasn't accidental? Must have got past me.'

'I suppose the reference to crime scene investigators being called in.'

'Oh, that. Harner certainly picked up on it.'

'He probably wasn't the only one. Well, shall we get to those papers of Follett's?'

*   *   *

Pedersen and Tate stood in the doorway to Max Follett's study.

'This,' said Pedersen, 'is going to be a bitch of a job.' From every flat surface drifts of paper confronted them. A four-drawer file cabinet was so tightly packed Tate had to tug hard with both hands to dislodge a single folder.

'I told you it was a mess,' Tate said. 'He hasn't even labelled the folders in the file cabinet. How the hell do you suppose he rounded up material to send to a publisher? Do you think he just crated it the way Thomas Wolfe is supposed to have done?'

Pedersen sighed. 'Who knows? Makes you understand why it took ten years to turn out that second book. He probably spent eight of them looking for pages of the manuscript. Well, might as well make a stab at it.'

Tate organized the task. It went better than they had expected. The stacks grew, the confusion on desk and table-tops diminished. Personal mail consisted primarily of invitations, most signed with feminine names. An occasional fan letter from some aspiring young writer turned up.

'Do you suppose he answered these notes?' Tate said.

'From the looks of it, he never answered anything. I just came across a dozen unopened letters, some of them invitations. One bill. Must have been a day he forgot to read the mail.' He picked up a notebook. 'No sign of the manuscript,' he observed.

'He wasn't totally without organization,' Tate pointed out. 'Look at this. He has one drawer just for the mimeographed material he gave out in class—course assignments, samples of edited pages, proofreader's symbols. I wouldn't have thought he'd have bothered, would you?'

'You think he'd just let the glory rub off on his students and skip the instruction? Talk about his own stuff a lot?'

'Maybe not. He was hard on students. He must have read their material.'

There was no sign of a will; however, two letters from Leona Morgan surfaced. One, undated, had apparently been left in the house; the other had been mailed.

The first was brief:

Max, I can't believe the *virulence* of your attack on me last night. I don't see how we can go on; what you said was an assault on the very essence of my being. How could you have gone on seeing me if you feel as you say? I can't even talk about it, I'm so so upset.

Leona.

The second, its envelope postmarked nine weeks earlier, expressed an entirely different spirit:

Max darling,

After last night, I felt marvellous about us. It's the first time you've let me see that you do have a commitment to our relationship, and I agree with you that we should marry. I understand your fears. You say four failed marriages should tell a man something. I've had only one failed marriage, but I know the feeling you're describing. Maybe what the four marriages should tell you is to be more sure this time.

The thing about us that's good is that we've had lots of time in which to make sure. I'm willing to take the chances you describe, although I feel you're exaggerating. The thing I won't risk is the one that's caused us all our trouble: other women. If we marry, the other women must *stop*. I mean that. This business of bedding every cute little undergraduate who bats her eyelids at you and tells you how wonderful your work is, and every matron who throws a party for you, will have to come to a halt. That's the condition if I'm to marry you. Is that agreed?

I also thought about the other things you said. You said it's up to me, you're willing to go along as we are or to marry, either way. I'm not willing. Actually, until we talked last night, I didn't realize how unwilling. At my age I need stability in my life, and at your age you certainly do. What I'm saying is that either we marry or we end things between us.

I hope it will be the former.

All my love,
Leona.

'Wow! Wonder when that first note was written. They weren't secretly married, you don't suppose?'

Pedersen shook his head. 'Doesn't sound as though she's looking for anything secret. I imagine public is what she wants.' After a moment he said, 'Could be he never wrote a will at all, just said that to shut his lawyer up.'

'He could have hidden it, really hidden it. Everybody says he was so paranoid.'

'His sister says she doesn't even know whether he had a safe-deposit box. We'll have to check on that.' Pedersen stretched. He was beginning to ache all over. 'I *hate* this sort of job.'

'Hey, we're almost done. Poor Dawn has to sort through this stuff in earnest. We should probably let her get at it soon, there are student writings here, short stories he hadn't turned back.' He surveyed the room. 'Let's each take half the stuff on that little table and that should do it.'

Pedersen was thoughtful. 'We haven't found that copy of the manuscript, either. I'm going to have the publisher express me a copy.'

Before leaving the house they checked the obvious hiding-places. Pedersen unearthed a manilla envelope filled with old photographs,

114

but no will. He put the photographs with the two letters he was taking.

'The will's in a safe-deposit box,' said Tate. 'It's got to be.'

'Or it doesn't exist.'

'You know,' Tate said, 'if it did turn out that Leona Morgan and Max Follett were married, she'd inherit. Doesn't a marriage invalidate previous wills?'

'You can be sure they didn't marry,' Pedersen said with conviction. 'The whole town would know it by now. How about if you drive?'

By the time they had locked the door and resealed the house, Pedersen's back had begun to throb and he found himself longing in the most craven way for nothing more than a hot bath. This afternoon he was aware of every one of his fifty-three years.

Tate pulled the car out, rounded the corner and started down the hill. As they passed the house with the orange door, he spoke. 'Do you think she's safe? Should we be doing something more?' His voice was anxious.

'What? Put a guard on the house? The department would love to finance that. I'll have a patrol car check regularly.'

'For what that's worth.'

'Yes.' Pedersen felt a sudden distaste for the case and everyone associated with it. He knew it was fatigue and would pass, and that he was being unfair. They all seemed decent people, concerned for each other, kind people actually. He sighed. It must be time for him to knock off. 'I'm finished for the day,' he said. 'It's four-thirty, anyway. How about you?'

Tate grinned, unaffected by their afternoon of sorting through the detritus of Max Follett's life. 'It's paperwork, always wipes you out. I don't know what you'd do without me.'

'You're right.'

'I'll work another hour. I have some things to line up for tomorrow. You haven't forgotten the little list we compiled yesterday?'

'You'll have to do it alone, Ron. I'm not going back. Just drop me at my car.' He was quiet for a moment; then he spoke. 'You know, Ron, I'm beginning to get the feeling that no one really—genuinely, I mean—*liked* this guy.'

'Yet they all went to that party for him. How do you figure that?'

'It's as though each of them thought he or she was the only one who felt distaste for the man. None of them was going to be the one who was vulnerable. And this deck business. Do you notice that they all act as though Follett had died from a fall into the ravine, rather than from a hair-drier dropped into the bathtub?'

'Yes. They took his saying he was pushed seriously, no matter how they protest.'

Pedersen sighed deeply. 'Tonight, you know, I feel like an old man.'

'You need a night's sleep.'

116

'Mmm.' He buried his left hand in his pocket and consoled himself by rolling the smooth surfaces of the jade between his fingers.

CHAPTER THIRTEEN

Keith's response to the destruction of the gazebo seemed barely credible to Karin.

He had got back from work late, almost five; Tuesday was student conference afternoon. He was pouring himself a beer when she told him.

'Do you mean to say,' she said, rising and walking to the other side of the room so she would not have to look up at him, 'that you think it's nothing? *Nothing?*'

'Now, Karin.' His voice was infuriatingly reasonable. 'I said no such thing. I said it was good it was just the gazebo. You never intended to build one when you started this project, so it's no great loss. Now if it had been the big house—'

'Do you know how long it took me to put that little extra nothing together?'

'I do. I feel bad about it, babe. You're misinterpreting—' At her expression, he changed course. 'You're edgy and upset. How could you think I'd treat your work as unimportant? Haven't I given you every encouragement?'

'As I give *you* every encouragement. But that you take for granted,' she said, her eyes

117

narrowed.

'Of course.' He sighed. 'We aren't going to make a women's issue of this, are we?'

That was too much for her. 'Goddamn you, Keith. You have no feeling, absolutely no feeling.' She turned and ran blindly from the room.

Keith moved to follow her; half way across the room he changed his mind. In the next room the silence was loud as the two children took in every word. Suddenly furious with Karin, he turned and slammed out of the house, banging the side door behind him resoundingly.

Half way up the hill he realized where he was heading.

*　　*　　*

Leona had been in her study; she waved vaguely at her desk and led him out to the deck. The sun hanging low beyond the still-broken railing was uncomfortably reminiscent. They glanced at each other without comment.

'So,' Leona said, seating herself and indicating a chair for him. 'What's happening down *your* way?' The question was tinged with bitterness. When he didn't answer, she went on more gently, 'I've been trying to make myself go down to Dawn's all day. She must be in a state. But then—' her voice faded a little—'I haven't been in such great shape myself.'

'I know.' Keith turned towards her. 'I never knew exactly what you and Max—' he paused, finding the right phrase—'meant to each other, were to each other, but I know this is hard on you.'

She laughed, a sharp sound in the quiet of the late afternoon. 'You aren't the only one who didn't know. Max was a strictly eat-your-cake-and-have-it man, a real bastard, if you want the truth.'

Keith's eyebrows shot up. She looked tense as a wire. One tense woman in a day was enough.

'You know,' she went on in the same taut voice, 'he was seeing or lusting after at least one other woman, usually two, ever since I've known him. Oh, the other woman changed and I remained the constant—that, I suppose, was to be my satisfaction. But this latest was too much. I'd have broken off with him altogether if he hadn't died first. Book or no book.'

That's candour, Keith thought. Being the leading lady in the script of the town's literary lion was a major consideration, and she didn't hesitate to come out with it. But it was not enough. Forthright snobbery amused him, just as covert snobbery would have turned him away from her.

'I'm surprised you had the party for him,' he said. 'Feeling the way you did.'

'We'd planned it, and I was damned if I was going to let anyone else know how I felt. I don't

119

even know why I'm telling *you*. Besides, everyone else liked Max.'

'You felt he had it coming to him?'

'The party?' She laughed. 'I guess so. He had some other things coming to him too, believe me.'

'Who,' he asked, half caring, 'was Max's new one? Anyone I know?'

'Marcie. Miss Single Mother Struggling to Hold Things Together. If ever the phrase "Butter wouldn't melt in her mouth" was made for anyone, it was made for Marcie.'

Indignation stirred in Keith. 'Hey, that's not fair. Marcie's OK. It's not her fault that Max was horny for every woman under thirty.'

'*Is* she under thirty? I doubt it.'

'You know what I mean. She certainly seems under thirty.'

'And what do I seem?'

'I don't know what you seem.' He sighed. 'I should have stayed at home. Karin was bitching at me and now you are. What's with the women in this town today?'

'Sorry. It's all nothing to do with you.'

'You heard,' Keith said, seizing the opportunity to change the subject, 'that somebody smashed some of Karin's work?'

'She called. Thank God it wasn't the Victorian house. Exactly what happened?'

'We don't know. We also don't know what it means. Pedersen, that detective, thinks maybe somebody has it in for both the Folletts.'

'Why on earth—'

'Nobody seems to know.'

'I don't like this.' She rose and began to pace the deck nervously.

He stood up and stopped her in her tracks. 'Leona, take it easy. You're upset, aren't you, really upset?'

'Well, of *course*.' Suddenly her face twisted. She leaned her head against him and, her voice muffled, said, 'I am. More than I ever thought I'd be. And scared.'

'Scared?' He put an arm around her and with his other hand tipped her chin up. 'Why scared?'

'This is something different. The other—oh, Keith, maybe we're *all* targets.'

'That's crazy. You're just undone by all this.' He continued to look down into the smoothly perfect face, made rosy by the warm afternoon light despite its unhappiness.

'Keith,' she said, and before he thought what he was about to do, he kissed her. A second later he thought: Jesus, what have I got myself into now?

WEDNESDAY

CHAPTER FOURTEEN

The photographs Pedersen had taken from the Follett house spanned all but the last years of

121

Max Follett's life. At some point Follett or someone else had arranged them in chronological order, probably in preparation for mounting in an album. Pedersen leafed through them, maintaining the order. Tate stood to one side of Pedersen's desk, looking on.

On the top was Max as a baby in the arms of his uncertain-looking mother. Then Max nude on his stomach, rearing up from a photographer's fur rug. Max as a curly-headed toddler, mother fondly looking on. A sturdy five- or six-year-old Max with lunchbox and cap, probably taken as he set off for a first day at school. A somewhat older Max and his father with fishing gear. The parents standing together before a large white frame house, the japonica bush beside them in full bloom, nervous smiles on their faces. Max, a solemn adolescent, staring down into a baby carriage.

The gap in age between the two children became more apparent as Max matured. In one snapshot Dawn stood to one side, her head ducked, her mouth set crossly, as though this undertaking most certainly was not her idea. Tate grinned.

Pedersen continued through the pictures. A professional photograph, Dawn as a pretty, shyly smiling teenager, perhaps her high school graduation picture. Max in his twenties with a young woman (his first wife?) in several shots taken at a beach, the couple intent on each other, the young woman's tilt of head flirtatious. More snapshots of them, then several of Max and another woman, Max with then a third. Finally several snapshots of Max and Florence, one taken at a party, his arm across her shoulders in an offhandedly possessive manner, a glass in his hand, in the background several people unrecognizable to Pedersen. Finally at the bottom of the packet, several professional photos of Max, perhaps taken for his first book jacket.

Nothing recent. No picture of Leona Morgan or of any of the Follett neighbours. It was as though a dozen years ago Max Follett had declared himself off bounds to friends with cameras.

Tate picked up one of the early snapshots. 'Reminds me of someone.'

Pedersen looked up. 'You know, that occurred to me, too. Probably just reminds us of Follett himself. He's been photographed so much by the press, we must know his face by heart.'

'No.' Tate put the picture down. 'It reminds me of someone else, I can't think who.'

'Dawn?'

'No. Someone else.' He picked up the picture. 'Who the hell does it remind me of?'

'Well, if you think who it is, let me know.' Pedersen suppressed a yawn. 'Sorry, I'm not awake yet. Freda put aside her ... resentment of me for a few minutes last night and gave me

123

a quick dinner and insisted I turn right in. She said I looked so tired it scared her. And by God, I slept right through, thirteen hours, six to seven.'

'She's still mad?'

'Not mad exactly, more depressed. Distant.' He sighed. 'Anything with the fingerprints?'

'Not a thing. A few of the girlfriend's and some of the sister's, but nothing else. Oh, a few smears, a few latents, probably the cleaning woman's. The sherry glass in the living-room was Dawn's. He gave her a drink when she dropped in Sunday.'

'Takes guts to keep alcohol around when you're a drinker,' Pedersen observed.

'I bet he'd be just the sort to pride himself on being able to do it.'

Pedersen sat thoughtful. 'I wonder about that will. From the shape of his affairs, I'd say nobody's going to come into a lot. Of course that may not be general knowledge.'

'The new book will bring something in, it's sure to be big. His death insures that.'

'You mean because he can't write another? Or because—'

'Yes, the publicity.' Tate grimaced. 'Just what every publisher hopes for, something sensational to put the book in the public eye. It'll sell like crazy.'

'Be that as it may, if he's left much to anyone other than his sister, that may give us a lead.'

'And a motive.'

'Yep. And if it all goes to Dawn, that could give her a motive. Except that she appears to be under attack as well.'

'I checked about that house patrol when I came in,' Tate said. He sat down in the room's other chair.

'You were busy this morning. I've been thinking, Ron. Florence Smith must know something about the Follett family. I'm going to drop by for a little talk with her this morning. While I'm there, I think I'll check next door and be sure things are calm at the Blochs'.'

'How about Dawn's?'

Pedersen raised his head and looked at the other man for a long moment. 'Sure, I'll stop by. While I'm out, why don't you see if you can dig up any newspaper interviews or magazine features that might tell us something?'

'If this is some vendetta, the newspapers and magazines may never have got wind of it.'

'Never can tell. They may have reported something without knowing its meaning. And Ron, just for the hell of it you might as well check and see if a marriage licence was issued to Follett in the past nine weeks.'

'You do think they might have been secretly married.'

'No, I meant what I said. I think she'd have shouted it to the world. But there's no harm in checking.'

*　　*　　*

Florence Smith was on her knees in the garden. She greeted Pedersen with something less than enthusiasm and thrust the pointed garden tool she was holding down into the earth. On the grass beside her was a little heap of dandelions she had already vanquished. 'Just let me get this, then I'll stop. Why don't you sit over there by the table?'

Pedersen eased back in the white wire chair, the early morning sun warm on his shoulders, and watched her work the weed free. Her garden reminded him of his grandmother's. In summer that had been a place of columbines and delicate nodding cosmos, massed zinnias and gaillardias; his strongest memory of his grandmother was of her dispatching him with shears and a basket and instructions to 'pick a good big bunch' for her daughter, his mother. A Freda sort of garden, it had been.

His own passion was for succulents. Tiny, slow-growing succulents were suggestive to him of some other planet, one in which the laws of nature and man were more precise, more in keeping with an order that encouraged rather than defeated life.

Small things, he had long ago recognized, attracted him. His diminutive wife, with no extra ounce of flesh, in contrast with his own bigness. The tiny worry beads. God, even the dwarfs in the peanuts.

126

Florence Smith washed her hands under the garden hose and pulled a chair near his. She sat down. 'Yes?' Her face was puzzled.

He smiled. 'I've been admiring your garden.'

'Doesn't look like me, does it?'

'Well—'

'Everybody's always surprised. I'm not what I look like. People just don't know me.' She looked around with satisfaction. 'And I *love* colour. But you didn't come here to talk about that.'

'Actually—you've talked with Mrs Bloch since yesterday?'

'You mean about the gazebo? Yes, she told me.'

'Any thoughts as to what that was all about?'

'Thoughts? No, not really. Karin tells me you have, though. You think somebody was getting at Dawn. I must say I can't see why, and it's a funny way to go about it.'

'That's why I'm here, Mrs Smith. We can't see why, either. We're hoping you may be able to help.'

She frowned. 'Me? How? What could I tell you that would help?'

'Maybe a great deal. You know your former husband's family, the sort of relations they had with people, whether there was someone who could have had it in for the whole Follett family.'

She threw a glance at him that indicated he

127

had unaccountably lost his mind. 'The *whole* family, what a queer idea. Why would anyone have it in for the Folletts? It's true I never met Max's parents, they'd both passed on, but everything he ever said about them made them sound like a Norman Rockwell calendar. The only thing at all unusual was the spacing between Max and Dawn and that was accident. Max's mother had a tubal pregnancy a couple years after Max was born and the doctor thought she shouldn't have more kids. Dawn just happened.'

'How about aunts, uncles, cousins?'

'Both Max's parents were only children.'

'Did your husband ever mention any member of the community who disliked the family—or disliked him and his sister? Or even disliked just the parents? Business rivalries or personal ones that could have led to strong feelings? An old boyfriend of Dawn's that the family disapproved of? Something at school?'

'I never heard a word of anything like that. Max and Dawn both did well in school, from what he said. He worked on the school paper, she was in the Dance Club. I can't see how any of that could lead to violent feelings.' She laughed. 'Of course Max may have antagonized people. He had pretty strong opinions. But not enough to make anyone take it out on Dawn, I shouldn't think.'

'Have you ever been to Longville?'

She looked surprised at his knowing the
128

name. 'Once. Max had to be up north one spring, something connected with his book, and I went along. While we were there, we drove to Longville—he wanted to show me the house he lived in as a kid. When we got there, he was all upset at how different it was. The family that had bought it had taken off the porch and re-landscaped. He fussed and fussed until he found that a big tree he remembered was still there and the japonica bush was alive.'

'Did you talk to neighbours? Or visit any old friends of your husband?'

'He stopped at the house next door—the parents' best friends had lived there. There were new people. We drove around town and finally stopped at a drugstore he knew. I had a cup of coffee at the fountain and he talked to the man who owned the place. He told Max most of his highschool friends had moved away. One Max was really fond of—I guess he and Max used to sit over Cokes in the drugstore and talk about all their plans for when they were grown up—was working for a news magazine. Billy Fitzgerald—the name just came to me. The drugstore man didn't have addresses, but Max thought maybe he'd write him where he worked.' She looked off over Pedersen's shoulder. 'He never did, though. He always thought he'd do things he never did.' She smiled. 'Like all of us.'

'You're sure he never reached him?'

'Unless he sneaked out and did it behind my

129

back.'

'What about Dawn? Was there ever family trouble over one of her boyfriends?'

'Here? Oh, you mean back then. Max wouldn't have known about that. He'd grown up and moved out long before she began going with boys. Of course, here, Max never much liked anyone she went around with. He was like an over-protective parent. When she got married, he stopped fussing over her. She told me that, Max didn't. But he never liked her husband.' She moved her chair so the sun didn't strike at her face. 'I've learned all that since Dawn moved here. By the time Dawn was married, Max and I had broken up.'

'You and Dawn are friends.'

She looked at him for a moment. 'I like Dawn. She's much nicer than her brother. Not that she thinks so, she liked him. I think she realized he was just being protective of her.'

Pedersen studied her for a moment. 'Tell me something, Mrs Smith. How did Max Follett react to your leaving him?'

She laughed. 'Let me tell you, he reacted all right. Max is very possessive of people, he hangs on for dear life.' Engulfing, Leona had told him. 'And the older he got, the less he liked change. He wanted things to stay just the way they were, no matter how bad they were. I can tell you he didn't make things easy for me.'

'But in the end...'

'In the end he had no choice. But he's kept

130

himself in my life, in some way, ever since. He really didn't let me go.' She waved impatiently. 'Let's not talk about it.'

Pedersen took out his notebook. 'What was the friend's name? Fitzgerald?'

'Billy Fitzgerald. Funny I remembered.'

Pedersen put away the notebook. 'Things straightened out with your husband?'

'You mean—about what I said? My abusing him? No.'

'You didn't tell him about meeting Max Follett on Saturday, did you?'

'No, I didn't.' She caught herself. 'Well, the cat's out of the bag now. I did lie to you. I met Max at the coffee house. I wanted to ask a favour of him and I didn't tell Arthur. I think he knew, though.'

'How was that?'

'I think from the way Arthur's acting that Max went by the nursery afterwards and told him we'd just had coffee together. He said, joking of course, that he was going to, but I didn't believe him. I thought his bark—' She stopped. 'Max was a vicious man. He probably told Arthur everything.'

'Everything. What do you mean by everything?'

'What we talked about, I mean, Max and I. He probably taunted Arthur, that's what it must have come down to.' She set her lips in a line and slid stiffly to the front edge of her chair, her feet flat on the bricks of the patio.

'We don't even know it's true.'

Pedersen had the odd feeling that somewhere he'd missed a beat. 'In what way did he taunt your husband?'

'With not being able to give me a baby.' In a rush of words, she added, 'We don't know if it's true, we've never been tested or even talked to a doctor about it. We—it was just Max being his usual vile self, but think how Arthur felt.'

'Where did Mr Follett get such an idea?'

'He seemed to think my *face* told him.' She laughed bitterly. 'Max knew how easily I became pregnant. After all, we were married for seven years.'

Pedersen looked around. 'You have children?'

'No!' Florence Smith stood up angrily. 'I don't, but it's not because I wasn't pregnant. So when Max asked me why we—Arthur and I—weren't having any, I must have looked ... funny. Anyway, he laughed and acted very knowing. And probably went to Arthur with his suspicions.' She kicked the base of the metal table, hard.

Pedersen asked, more to comfort her than for information, 'You did explain to your husband that you'd said nothing.' God, he thought, hearing himself, I sound like somebody's family counsellor. He closed off the topic. 'I'm sure he understood it was just malice.'

'No. I haven't talked with him about it. And

he won't understand. Max is the one person Arthur has always been jealous of. I can't tell you the time I've spent trying to make him understand that our marriage is completely different. He feels—felt—I still thought about Max too much, that I wasn't really free of him. Do you think that's true, that even if you're having bad thoughts about somebody, you're involved with him?'

Pedersen was not about to be lured into this trap. 'It's something you and your husband will have to talk out, I think.' He paused. 'You know, when I originally spoke to you, I didn't have the impression you were so bitter about him. Why did you go to the party for him Saturday night?'

'I'm the only one that feels—felt—that way about Max. Everyone else liked him. I wasn't going to give him the satisfaction of seeing I felt that way. I never gave him that satisfaction, I was always very matter-of-fact with him.'

'But your husband. It surprises me that he'd go near the man if he was just in his shop taunting him, as you think he was.'

She sighed and looked down at her hands. 'I think Arthur must feel the same way I do. We weren't going to give him the satisfaction of thinking he'd got to us.' She looked up. 'This is a terrible thing to say, but...'

'Yes?'

'I'm almost glad he's dead.'

* * *

Next door the Bloch house was silent and serene. There was no sign of activity in or around the house nor was there any sign of life towards the back of the property where Marcie Terpstra lived. Pedersen circled the house. The screen had been replaced, the scuffed area beneath it raked neatly.

* * *

Although he had not planned to visit her, in fact had intended to continue directly on down the road to Dawn's, on impulse Pedersen strolled around the corner. Perry's study window faced the street; he could see her inside, bent over her word-processor, intent. He had never warmed to those machines, although by now all business was conducted on them. He wished instead that he heard typewriter keys clacking; somehow it seemed more writerly to him. But he walked up the path and rang the doorbell.

Away from the study window now, he imagined her rising with an impatient gesture. In a moment she appeared at the open door. 'Detective? You've come back for more?' Distraught when he had first glimpsed her, she now appeared contained, at ease. She was a handsome woman, he noted, with her close-cropped white hair, her aristocratic bearing.

'Just a word or two.' He followed her in. 'I'm interrupting you.'

'It'll be there when I get back.' She led him into the living-room. It was a pleasant room furnished with unremarkable, comfortably worn pieces that lent a look of easy domesticity. A bowl of fresh flowers on a table was a dash of bright colour. 'May I get something for you? Coffee? Tea?'

'No. Thanks, but I won't keep you that long. I just wanted to inquire into the— relationships, I guess you'd call them, in the neighbourhood.'

'I hate that word,' she said.

He was startled. 'Why?'

'Everybody uses it these days to suggest—oh, I don't know. It just doesn't seem to have the connotation it used to. It's like *share*. *Share* this with me,' she mocked. 'Actually,' she laughed. 'I don't particularly want to share with you the nature of the neighbourhood relationships, but I suppose I will.'

'I know what you mean about *share*.' He grinned. 'Now if you'll just let me know where you're coming from...'

She laughed. 'That's the other one. I don't think I'm made for California.'

'I doubt that it's just California. Where are you from?'

'Michigan, the great Midwest. I suppose Michiganders are sharing things too—and

135

having relationships.'

'Which brings us back—'

'Yes. What relationships exactly is it that you want to know about?'

'Let's start with Max and his former wife. And her husband.'

'Florence and Arthur. I certainly don't think they sought out Max, but they all got along—civilly, I'd say. They ran into each other all the time. We're a neighbourly bunch and Max was one of the neighbours.'

'Yes, I've noticed that. So you saw no particular antagonism, despite past history.'

She shrugged. 'If it was there, they handled it.'

'And the Blochs and Max?'

'They were friends. You have to understand about Max. He didn't entertain. I mean, he didn't give dinner parties or backyard barbecues or anything of that sort. He dropped in on people.'

'And they on him?'

'Well, some. Mostly Leona or Dawn. The rest of us had been given to understand that when he was writing he was strictly incommunicado. He wrote from about nine to three.'

'And after three?'

'I really think it was Max who did the after-three dropping in.'

'He came here?'

'Not often. We weren't particular friends. I

136

don't mean we were—what did you say the other day, enemies?—it's just that there was a professional antagonism. You can understand that. He had trouble producing; I produced, but I didn't get any critical kudos. And he didn't—' She changed her mind.

'He didn't?'

'Well, it's neither here nor there, but he wasn't too fond of the woman I lived with.' A spasm of pain crossed her face. 'She died a year and a half ago. Cancer.' After a pause she said, 'A long, dragging death.'

'I am sorry. That must have been difficult for you.'

'Awful. I thought afterwards I should have held on to her, clutched her—physically, I mean, somehow made her fight. She just lay there and—gave in.' She looked at him. 'I've thought often of Thomas's poem since.'

'Thomas's poem?'

'Dylan Thomas. "Do not go gentle into that good night." You should read it sometime.'

'I will. But I'm sure ...'

'Oh, you're right. There was nothing I could have done, not really. And she was in pain. Terrible pain.' After a while she returned her glance to his as though she had just remembered her was there. 'What was it you were asking me?'

'You had just said Max Follett didn't like your companion.'

'He never said anything. He just looked at us
137

as though we were something contemptible. It's hard to pinpoint, but there was no question what he was feeling.'

'Yet you liked him well enough to go to a party for him.'

'He—sort of made amends. When she got sick, I think he was really sorry he'd been so—whatever he was. He came to see her, he brought flowers and books, he tried. I got over my anger at him. Besides, I was the only one in the neighbourhood who had any bad feelings about him. Everyone else liked him. I wouldn't have spoiled his little triumph over something from the past.' It was clear, though, that she still had feelings; her face was taut with emotion. But, Pedersen thought, looking at her, that may just be because she's been talking about her friend.

'So you were the only one who had reason to dislike him. What about the others? Leona?'

'I guess he gave her problems with other women, but she seemed to take that in stride. I'd say she was deeply attached to him.'

'And—who else is there? Marcie? Dawn?'

'He was Marcie's teacher, that's all. Her neighbour. Dawn, of course, thought he was God himself.'

'She was that attached?'

'Well, maybe not lately. She's been doing some growing up. She seems more balanced about everything, including Max. But she used to just adore the ground he walked on. I don't mean she didn't have spats with him; she had times when she'd be furious with him over something. I guess the worst was back when she was married. Max never thought much of her husband, or so I gather. But he left her alone about it after a while. I think, in all, Dawn loved her brother a lot. He was like a father to her in some ways.' She glanced towards the window. 'Probably not as difficult as some fathers.'

'Yours?'

She looked at him coldly. 'Among others.'

'So you all went to that party Saturday night feeling happy for Max. Pleased about his success.'

'I think so. Of course I was mildly jealous, but I know my limits and I've long since learned to live with them. But I think we were all quite in the spirit of the thing—really there to celebrate his success.'

As he rose to go, Pedersen reflected. How many people was it now who had said, Everyone liked Max, I was the only one who didn't? Arthur? Had Florence said it? Perry? Somehow he had the impression that everyone at that Saturday night party had had a bone to pick with Max, everyone had thought: I'm the only one, I'll be a good sport. Or: I won't give him the satisfaction. It was a disquieting impression.

*   *   *

On the way down the road to Dawn's, he once again passed the Bloch house and thought how serene it appeared. Dawn was at home, but a glance told him things in this household were not serene. She opened the door cautiously, just a few inches, then when she saw it was he, swung it wide. Her face was strained.

'What is it, Dawn?'

'Oh, I'm so glad you came, Detective Pedersen! You got my message.'

'Message? No.'

'Come in, I have to show you something.' Her voice was thick.

He could see nothing in the studio that did not look exactly as it had on his previous visit. 'What? What is it you want to show me?'

'This.' She led him to the worktable and lifted a towel. It covered a crushed and twisted lump of drying clay.

'The piece you were working on? I don't understand. You dropped it?'

'I didn't drop it. I *found* it like this. I went for my morning walk and when I came back I saw it on the floor under the table. Somebody must have got in here and deliberately destroyed it. Maybe it even happened last night when I was asleep and I just never noticed till this morning.' Tears began to slide down her face. 'I'm scared. I don't know what it means.'

Pedersen walked to the door and checked the lock. 'You've got to change this. Anybody

140

can get in, all he'd need is a piece of plastic. A credit card.' He walked back and stood before her.

'I don't know what it means,' Dawn said again, her voice small.

Pedersen looked down at the twisted lump of clay which lay on the table. It means, Dawn, he thought, that somebody's trying to get a message to you. He glanced at the white face beneath the mop of curls. And I don't like it. I don't like it at all.

*　　*　　*

'You did stay with her till the locksmith came?' Tate's question was accusing.

'No, but he was on his way. You like her, don't you, Ron?'

Tate walked to the window and stood, back to Pedersen, gazing out at the gingko tree. It was a clear, bright day; the summer fog had already burned off. 'I'm sorry for her. And all these things that are happening to her worry me.' He turned and added fiercely, 'We don't need any more accidents.'

'It worries me too, Ron. These minor assaults could precede something more serious. Before I left today, I tried to feel out whether she knew of anyone at all who could have it in for them simply because they're Folletts—Voletskis, whatever. I didn't want to scare her, so I soft-pedalled it. But she didn't

141

seem to know what I was talking about.'

'Could Dawn be the real target? If it were her former husband, for example. Although—'

'Somehow I think it's both of them. Anything on the biographical check?'

'Just a beginning. Ordinary Middle American family. Uneventful childhood. Some wild oat sowing in college. And a lot of stuff on his many marriages.'

'Anything recent enough to refer to Leona Morgan?'

'No. Most of the stories date around the time of his first book. The later ones go into why some writers are prolific and others take forever to write each book. Discussions of Flaubert.' He shrugged. 'Follett's hardly in a category with Flaubert.'

'Did Flaubert take a long time over his books?'

'Days over a page. A paragraph. Weeks.'

Pedersen digested the information without comment. 'And Follett's bank? Did he have a safe-deposit box?'

'They say not. Just the checking account and CDs.'

'That doesn't make sense. We didn't find the house papers when we went through his stuff. No marriage certificates or divorce papers. Not even homeowner's insurance. Where in hell could he have stashed all that stuff?'

'There are other banks.'

'But why? Why not use the convenient one,

the one he deals with every day?'

'He was a queer guy. Paranoid, all his friends say.'

'He certainly was queer.' Pedersen's disgust was reflected in his tone. 'Well, we'll have to try to nose out his little hiding-places.'

* * *

Freda had left a message for him to call by noon. Instead, on an impulse, he got in his car and headed for the pizzeria. As he drove home the closed box on the seat beside him filled the car with the fragrance of cheese and mushrooms.

For the first time in several days she greeted him with a smile. 'You brought lunch! I haven't had pizza in weeks.' She transferred it to a favourite Italian platter he had given her and got out plates and tablemats. 'There's even coffee ready. You got my message?'

'Yes. What's up?' Her mood seemed too upbeat for it to be more trouble with her mother.

'You'll never guess. I was cast as Olga! Olga, remember, the interesting older woman? *Not* the mother, for a change.' Freda had bemoaned the fact that she was perennially cast as the mother in The Players' productions. She laughed with delight.

He realized how much he had missed hearing that laugh. 'Wonderful! You'll be

143

good.'

'Of course I will. I've been telling them. It's made all this with my mother seem easier to take.' She sobered. 'I had a call from Clara today.'

'What did she say?' He helped himself to a large wedge of pizza.

She sat down opposite him and served herself. 'She says Mother's afraid to go to sleep at night. She wants Clara or one of the kids to come over and sit with her, hold her hand.' She shook her head. 'It's awful, Clara has enough without that. You know, Carl, it's just not like Mother, she's always been so independent.'

'Like her daughter.'

She was quiet for a few minutes. 'Do you think it'll happen to us? I'll be asking Carrie to hold my hand?'

That's the fear, he thought. That's why I haven't listened when Freda tried to talk to me about her mother. That's why the whole subject depresses me. I'm afraid, too.

He kept his eyes on her face. 'She was independent for a very long while, remember. But she was never eighty before. She never had cancer before. You know, you're feeling guilty again. You said you wouldn't.'

'I do feel guilty. It isn't fair, Clara's having to do it all. She's *my* mother, too. It's no wonder Clara—'

He stopped her. 'Freda. Clara doesn't want your mother dead. And we've offered to have

144

her. She hates California and she doesn't want to leave her friends or her house. And Clara's kids. She's seen them every day of their lives.'

'We have kids. What about Matt and Carrie?'

'What are you talking about? Neither of them is here. Even if she were with us, she wouldn't see them. After all, you were with her when she had the surgery. And you help financially. What more can you do?'

Gloom had descended again. She refused to look at him.

He leaned forward and took her hands. 'Look, try not to worry. Your mother's just been through a difficult period, she's scared. After this play is over, maybe we should talk about your going east to see her again. It might help you get things in perspective.'

She fixed her gaze on the table. 'Maybe.'

'Come on, sweetie.' He grinned. 'Don't pout.'

Despite herself, she laughed. 'I want to pout. It makes me feel better.' She got up and came around the table to kiss him. 'No more pizza for me. I'm off to a Players meeting.' She kissed him again. 'Thanks,' she said. 'Thanks.'

As he finished his second cup of coffee and the remains of the pizza, he thought of what she had said earlier: *Was Max Follett in someone's way, like Mother?* What then, of Dawn—was she also in someone's way? An unfamiliar pang of anxiety touched him. He

145

had better find out, before she was no longer around to be in anyone's way.

CHAPTER FIFTEEN

The phone call came in the afternoon. Dawn's voice was low. 'Detective Tate, I just wanted to tell you the key turned up. The missing key to my brother's house.'

'Oh.' He was sure the relief he felt was evident in his voice. 'Good. It was just mislaid, then.'

There was a little silence at the other end. Then, in the same laboured voice, she spoke again. 'Not exactly. I found it in that bowl, the place where I usually keep it. Remember?'

'Could you have—'

'I don't see how. Detective Pedersen and I both looked there. And I looked when you were here.'

'You've had your locks changed? Deadbolts put in?' He was shocked at the sense of panic that had arisen in him.

'Yes. Maybe it's just me. Maybe I put the key there and forgot.'

'Look.' He put aside his misgivings at his own reaction. 'I'll run out there. I have to check something else with you, anyway. You'll be there for a while?'

'Yes.' Her voice lightened. 'Thank you. I'm a little ... frightened.'

The drive took ten minutes. The house with its cheerful, gaudy door, its warped fence, did not suggest malevolence.

She answered the door immediately, as though she had been waiting. Although she wore what he thought of as her uniform, bright tights and shirt and today a long, clay-smudged jumper, her hair was for the first time uncombed and her face drawn. Today she looked her age.

'I'm glad you're here.' She bolted the door after him. I must—' she tried for a light laugh—'be more scared than I think. I've been sleeping badly. Nightmares. People chasing me. Last night—' she shuddered—'it was a dog, a great hairy, snarling thing.'

He knew and as rapidly repressed the thought that he wanted to take her in his arms and comfort her. He brushed the grey kitten from a chair and seated himself as far as possible from her.

She was working hard to maintain calm. 'Can I get you something?' She held out her hand to the kitten. 'Here, Muffin.'

He smiled. 'Sleepytime tea? No, nothing. Now tell me, did you give anyone the key to your new lock?'

'Just my landlord, he's not going to come in. He has to have it in case of fire—you know, we have a kiln, *he* has a kiln and I use it. And he needs a key in case I drop dead or something.' She could not smile at the ludicrousness of the

147

idea. He could hear her thinking: Or am murdered.

He walked over to the door. 'Are you *sure* you locked it?'

'I'm sure. I've been feeling a little uneasy. I double-checked.'

'And the windows?'

'I think—'

'You *must* lock both your windows and doors, Dawn.' He enunciated the word with the severity of an anxious father. 'And have your landlord put on a chain—*today*. Let's see the bowl with the key.'

The bowl was a small one. The key all but filled it. There was no possibility it had been overlooked in the original search.

'Look, if it'll make you feel better to be doing something, go ahead and make some tea. I'll talk to you while you do it. I had planned to get in touch with you today.'

She rose and went to the kitchen end of the room. Her tea-kettle was the same bright red as her skirt. It struck him that there was a sort of bravery—or bravado—in her use of colour.

'You checked the rest of the place to see if anything else was touched?' he asked.

'No. I came in from the grocery store and saw the key and phoned you. Should I have?'

'It's a good idea. While you make the tea, I'll look around.'

Nothing seemed to have been disturbed. The piece she had been working on was neatly covered. Plates and cups stood in their places. Books were on shelves. Maybe she had imagined an intruder, had somehow missed the key the first time round. He strolled to the closet, swung open the door and stopped. 'Dawn,' he said.

'Yes,' she called.

'Come here.' He heard her set down the kettle, then her footsteps as she neared the place where he stood.

'My God,' she said softly.

The clothing in the closet had been slashed with a knife or scissors. The garments hung in rags.

'My God,' she said again. 'everything I own. What'll I wear?'

The kitten rubbed against his leg and Tate jumped, suddenly furious. 'That's not the question, the question is who in hell did this?'

In a responsive anger she said, 'Well, *my* question is what I'm going to have to put on.' She walked to the dresser and opened a drawer. 'They left this stuff. Or—' she added with bitterness—'saved it for next time.'

Tate turned to her. 'Your landlord probably has insurance that'll cover you. You can buy new clothes, but—I don't like this, I don't like it at all.'

'Well, I'm not exactly wild about it myself.' She thrust a hand into the closet. 'He missed a couple of items. I may not have to go naked after all.'

'You poor kid.' Tate stood before her. 'Let's get the tea. We need it now.'

In the kitchen she removed the kettle from the little stove and reached for a box of tea. 'You wanted to ask me something.'

'Yes. Did your brother ever talk to you about a will, Dawn? Did he tell you he'd written one or give any hint as to where he kept it?'

'No.' She stopped. 'Actually, he did once. He said if anything happened to him the house would be mine, that he'd had the mortgage insured so it would come to me without any liens. His telling me was funny. You know—' she smiled—'my brother was a pretty strange guy. He never talked about things like that, never confided anything. I think he didn't trust even me. Only that once. He didn't mention a will, though.'

'He told his lawyer he had hand-written one; the lawyer was apparently worried about it. The royalties on the first book must be substantial and your brother was approaching fifty. The lawyer thought it was cavalier of him to leave the issue of the inheritance unresolved.'

'Max knew I wasn't worrying about it. And if it had been left unresolved it would eventually all have come to me, anyway, wouldn't it? Isn't that the way it works?'

'Yes, but it's more complicated and takes time.'

'Well—' she shrugged—'I thought it was good of Max to do that, insure the mortgage, but I'm perfectly fine right here. At least I was till all these things began happening.' She swung around. 'Do you think somebody's going to ... kill me?' Her eyes on him were intent. Tate took an involuntary step towards her.

He checked himself. 'No! We'll *see* to it that nothing happens to you. Dawn, I think you should consider staying with friends for a while. Won't the Blochs or Marcie put you up?'

'Marcie? She has no space for me. No, I want to stay here. If someone's after me, it won't matter where I am. Look what happened to the gazebo. That wasn't here, that was in the Blochs' house.'

'Then you must be meticulous about locking windows and doors. And get that chain today. You hear me? I'd suggest a burglar alarm, but I suppose that would be too big an expense for you.'

'It would.' She smiled. 'Let's wait to see if I really do inherit anything from Max before I start getting big ideas.' She poured boiling water over the tea. 'You know, I keep expecting him to walk in, just to appear at the door the way he used to and say, "What are you up to, kid?"' She laughed uneasily.

'I think that's a natural reaction, Dawn.'

'Probably. But it's as if he's ... haunting me.' She turned to him, her face puzzled.

151

He smiled. 'I don't think that's quite the word. But I have heard that people feel the presence of a—person long after he's gone. He'll probably be around for a while, I imagine.'

He left her holding Muffin close and looking anxious. He heard the bolt slide into place after him.

Driving away from her and back to headquarters, Ronald Tate allowed himself a few forbidden notions as to what he would do when this was over. They were the first such thoughts he had contemplated with seriousness since the day his divorce became final.

CHAPTER SIXTEEN

Perry was so deeply absorbed in what she was doing that it wasn't until the second tap at the window that she turned her head. For a moment she was not just startled but afraid. Then she realized who it was and rose to go to the door.

'Leona, why are you creeping around like that?' She stood back so the other woman could enter.

'I rang and rang. Does your doorbell work?'

'Oh Jesus.' She reached to check it. 'The damned thing's been acting up, but I thought I'd fixed it.' She turned to her guest. 'This is a nice surprise. Can I fix you a cup of coffee?'

'Would you?'

'I should stop, anyway. I've done enough for one day. Come on out to the kitchen.'

'I've meant to call,' Leona said, perching on a stool alongside the counter. 'I felt terrible about your finding Max like that. But—well, I was dealing with some feelings of my own.'

'Of course you were. I should have called you. I've thought of it, but—'

'But you knew things were pretty much over for Max and me?'

Perry measured out the coffee, filling the little plastic scoop precisely and watching the dark granules sift into the basket. She had given the same care to filling the pot. She could feel Leona's eyes hard on her. Leona was waiting for an answer.

'To tell the truth, I never knew how things were between you and Max.'

'You saw me over there often enough, you must have had some idea.' The voice was mildly resentful, as though she had been slighted by Perry.

Perry shrugged. 'I didn't pay much attention to what went on over there. Except, of course,' she added, remembering, 'in the morning. We couldn't help noticing each other then, with our windows the way they are.' She plugged in the coffee-pot.

Leona got off the stool and walked to the window that faced the Follett house. 'You can't see who goes in and out.'

'No.' Perry glanced at her back. 'I can't even see the front path from here. Those bushes cut it off, the oleanders.'

Leona swung around. 'But you probably hear things. With windows open, you must hear things.'

'Leona, I'm working most mornings—was there something in particular I should have heard?'

'Of course not. I just—you said you didn't know about Max and me.' She returned to her stool and changed the subject. 'What did you think about all that ... interest in the party Saturday night? That Detective Pedersen came to talk to me about it.'

'They think he's been murdered.' Perry's voice was flat.

Leona looked up, startled. 'They *told* you?'

'Of course not. Why should the police tell me anything? It's obvious they don't think it was an accident.'

'But suicide...'

'I think they took seriously that business of Max's thinking he was pushed.' She reached into the china cupboard for mugs.

'That's ridiculous! You didn't see anyone push him, did you?'

'Not that I'm conscious of.'

'Who was close to him when he fell? Arthur, wasn't he?'

'Arthur. You were, too. And Marcie had

154

just been talking with Arthur when the rain blew in.'

'My!' Leona pursed her lips. 'You're the regular little detective. How could you notice all that in the confusion of getting things indoors? I certainly don't remember that clearly.'

Perry looked at her levelly. 'Whatever you think of my books, I'm a writer. Writers are observers.'

'Of course.' Leona came over, picked up a mug and turned it in her hands. 'Don't be offended. And I ... well, I haven't really read any of your books. I don't read a lot, I'm so busy, but I hear your books are good. Very good. The *Banner* certainly thought so.'

'Good within the genre. They weren't quite as unconditional as you're being.'

'Your publisher certainly sells a lot of them. You must make a lot of people happy.'

The percolator had stopped sputtering. Perry poured the dark liquid into the mugs. 'Shall I put out something? A cookie, maybe?'

Leona shook her head with vigour. 'No, I never eat sweets. I can gain pounds just looking at a piece of cake.' She picked up her mug. 'Good.'

'Not wonderful. I just don't have time to fuss with a filter pot. Now, what's on your mind, Leona? You seem to think I should have noticed something I didn't, something about Max.'

155

Leona set her mug down, a little shakily. 'No, no, Perry. It's just that we—that little group that was with him Saturday—we seem to be in the limelight. I understand that Pedersen has talked to every one of us. What do they think, for God's sake? That we came over here and slung that drier in his tub or something?'

'Probably that's just what they do think. It's uncomfortable, I know. And since you've brought it up, will you be put out if I ask what *was* going on between you and Max? You've been seeing him for over two years, haven't you? I assume you haven't just been discussing literature, but what about this business of things being over between you? Why did you give that party if things were all over?'

'I don't mean we weren't speaking, nothing like that. And I was pleased, Perry. He'd worked at it so long and had such trouble with that novel. How could I not have a party for him?'

'So what you meant is that you just weren't a romantic item any longer.'

Leona's laugh was bitter. 'Romantic? There never was anything *romantic* about Max's and my relationship, believe me. But I'd had it. He couldn't decide whether what he wanted was me or me and sixteen other women. I was fed up.' She raised her hands to the smooth hair. 'I didn't have to take that, not endlessly I didn't.'

'So you gave him an ultimatum.'

156

Leona laughed; it was a sharp, humourless sound. 'One of many. For what it was worth. At any rate, it was the final ultimatum. He knew.'

Perry looked at the smooth face of her guest. 'Then,' she said, 'it isn't as hard for you, Max's death. You'd already ... disengaged yourself emotionally.'

Leona's hands smoothed the dark hair and resmoothed it. 'It is hard,' she said. 'You know, I think I never stopped hoping. But I was fed up. I wouldn't have endured any more. I had to bring things to an end.' She covered her mouth, aware of what she had said. 'I don't mean—'

'Of course not.' Perry's face felt stiff. 'More coffee, Leona? How are things going with the new museum show?'

Leona Morgan thrust out her cup, her relief at the change of topic transparent. 'Fine,' she said. 'Just fine. Everything at the museum's fine.'

*　　*　　*

Tate had calculated in terms of Max's impatience. Twenty miles seemed like a reasonable distance for an impatient man to be expected to travel in indulgence of a personal eccentricity. Accordingly, Tate had dispatched a bulletin to every bank within twenty miles of Bay Cove.

The call, when it came, was from Lewistown.

The switchboard put it through.

'Mr Follett did have CDs with us, Detective. And a safe-deposit box.'

Midweek was a quiet time for the Bank of Lewistown. The lines of mortgage-payers, singles dropping by for weekend spending money and workers depositing pay cheques during lunch-hours that characterized Friday's bank activities were replaced by a desultory depositor or two, a housewife urging along a reluctant toddler, a boy in jogging clothes. Tate arrived with the order to open just before three. At the entrance to the vault he was met by one of the two bank officials who were to supervise the activity. In the absence of the key the box would have to be broken into, destroyed.

The destruction took place with remarkable efficiency. As Tate and the officials watched, the bank's mechanic applied a drill. In a moment of shrill sound the box was opened.

The bank officials stood by to tabulate the contents. The box contained what Tate might have expected. Papers relating to the purchase of the house, a birth certificate, a homeowner's policy, a bundle of commemorative Kennedy dollar bills, a mortgage insurance policy on his property on Glenvale Road, three certificates of deposit. A thin rubber-banded bundle contained marriage certificates, divorce papers. There was no marriage more recent than his and Florence's. But there was a blue-bound will.

Tate unfolded it. It was not hand-written, but had been drawn up two months earlier by a Lewistown lawyer. It named Doris Follett as executor, left his house and ten thousand dollars to her. His copyrights and the balance of his estate, which appeared to be well over two hundred thousand dollars, he had left to someone else.

He had bequeathed them to Kevin Terpstra.

* * *

Once more in her own house, Leona Morgan was on the phone. 'I do think you should,' she was saying with an earnestness unfamiliar even to herself. 'I can't make it and one of us should be at that meeting tomorrow. Just to find out how they'll use your Victorian house and whether there's anything more you'll need to do. They don't even know there's to be no gazebo. Unless you've told them. I haven't.'

'If I must, I will,' Karin said. 'But you know it's Keith's free afternoon. We have half a dozen errands we were planning to run. Keith was going to take Ricky for new gym clothes and I told Ellie we'd stop at the library. And we were all going out to dinner. How late do these things run?'

'Never past four. Your kids won't be home from day camp till three, anyway, will they? You'll still have time for your errands.'

'Not all. Keith and I—oh hell, I'll go to the damned thing. You don't think they're going to ask me to start on another gazebo?'

'No, no, of course not. They never actually asked for it in the first place. It was your and Dawn's idea.'

'Is there anything I should know? Will the museum director be there?'

'Yes. You know him. He'll make you comfortable. I phoned and said you were standing in for me since they were planning to discuss the September show. You're an *angel*, Karin. Thanks.' Before Karin could protest further or follow up with additional questions, she rang off.

Of course Leona had known it was Keith's afternoon off. And there was no real obstacle in the way of her attending the meeting, none but her impatience. Since the moment Keith had stepped close and kissed her, she had thought of him. The night before, lying awake in bed with her window open to the bay air, she told herself it was a reaction, just a response to the loss of Max and the frightening emptiness that had engulfed her since then. Perhaps it was only that. Perhaps the impulse that had moved Keith to kiss her and then depart in such guilty haste had been no more than a response to her beauty. She was aware of its effect. But—or so it now seemed to her—there had been a tension, a sexual awareness between herself and Keith from the moment they had met at that first neighbourhood meeting. And she wasn't about to lure him from his wife and children, she was merely—well, she wasn't sure exactly what.

Perhaps just seeing him, confirming that what she had perceived was a fact, was all she wanted. Tomorrow afternoon would give her that opportunity.

*   *   *

'It means just what you think it does,' Pedersen said. 'It means Kevin Terpstra is his son.'

'But she barely knew the guy. She took his class and dropped out. That was it.'

'Not quite. That's what she *told* us. But there must have been a little something more, a visit to his house to pick up a paper, a drink after school, something. Maybe it was a one-shot affair, but I can't think of another reason for that bequest. Can you?'

Ronald Tate shook his head. 'I guess not. Funny she didn't tell us. After all, he was dead...'

'That's why she didn't tell us. Would you identify yourself with a man who has just died under mysterious circumstances?'

'Which means she didn't know about the inheritance. If she'd known what was in his will, she'd have known we'd find out soon enough.'

'Maybe. Why don't you go up and talk to

her in the morning—and to Dawn, too? See how they react to the news. I think I'm going to take a run up to Longville—it's not more than four hours' drive. By the time I get back that manuscript should be here.'

'I will.' Tate looked at Pedersen thoughtfully. 'What are you looking for—up there, I mean?'

'I'm not sure. Someone who knew the family. Maybe just the ambience. I really won't know till I get there.'

'And this Marcie business. This adds one to our list of suspects, doesn't it?'

'*Adds* one? Everyone who was at that deck party is a suspect and has been from the beginning. This just clarifies the motive of one of them.' He looked at his partner. 'I grant you that they all seem like decent people, but they're suspects too, Ron. Don't forget that for a minute.'

CHAPTER SEVENTEEN

Florence Smith had never thought of her husband as a subtle man. One of Arthur's attractions for her, after seven years of a man like Max Follett, was his directness, what she thought of as his sweet simplicity.

By Wednesday afternoon of the week of Max's death she had revised her opinion. In the past three days Arthur had manifested an ingenuity at avoidance that she would never have believed possible of him had she not witnessed it. If she hadn't known him so well, known the tension he must be feeling in this unfamiliar role, she might have given up. Instead, she decided, no two ways about it, she would have to force a confrontation. She did something that in other circumstances she might never have considered: she went to the nursery and threatened to make a scene.

Arthur, for some reason—well, actually she knew the reason—detested scenes. He had told her early in their marriage that the one thing he sought was peace. Just peace. Knowing she would be there when he came home. Knowing dinner would be served on time. Knowing the house would be bright, cheerful. 'Not,' he had explained, 'that I'm asking you to become a domestic drudge. If you want to work, you should work. If you want to study, do that. But...' Here he had sat quiet for several minutes. 'What I would like is a household different from the one I grew up in. I'll do anything I can, anything you want of me, I'll meet you half way, but—' She had interrupted him. After Max it was what she wanted, too. And with occasional interludes that distressed them both, it had been like that.

Arthur was in the greenhouse when she arrived. She asked one of the clerks to let him know she was there. Then she went into his office and sat down behind his desk.

163

She could see that he was angry, angry with a cold rage she had never before seen in him. He stood in the doorway. His voice low, he said, 'What exactly is this?'

'I came to talk.'

'Here? You came to talk here?'

'Yes. We can close the door.'

He glared at her.

'Close it, Arthur. We can't go on like this.' God, she thought, I sound like a soap opera.

He reached behind him and pushed the door shut. His lips formed a hard white line. 'Talk.'

She stiffened. 'No matter how angry you are, you needn't speak to me like that.'

With one foot through the rung, he pulled a chair towards him. He sat down heavily. '*Please* talk, then.'

'Arthur. What are you so furious about? What have I done to you?'

'Nothing. Not one single thing.'

'You act as though you hate me.'

He wiped a hand across his face. 'I don't hate you.'

'Max told you what he *assumed* about our— our ability to have a baby. I never told him anything. I wouldn't tell him anything. You know that. Max was an evil man. He destroyed people.'

'A little melodramatic, don't you think?'

'No, I don't. That is what he did. That's why he was killed.'

'That's what you think?'

'That's what I know.'

He looked at her for a long moment. 'Why did you meet him that Saturday? What was there about it that you had to lie to me?'

'It wasn't anything to lie about.' She leaned forward. 'I lied—that is, I didn't tell you about it, because you've always been so funny about Max.'

'Funny. I've been *funny*?'

'That's the wrong word. I know you hate—hated—him and were ... jealous. I went to see him about library business, honestly, Arthur. It was my vanity. I was afraid he'd turn us down and I thought ...'

'You could seduce him into speaking at the library.'

'Arthur. *Please*.' She held out her hands to him. 'I knew him. I figured he was a writer, after all. Writers care about libraries. I thought I could make him see what a drawing card he'd be and ... well, we were going to rent the civic auditorium and charge for the talk. Raise some money. The library's always so short on books, equipment, everything. We thought the Friends would be making a real contribution.'

He lowered his voice further. 'Somehow all this does not seem the sort of thing to lead to a discussion of conception.'

'We didn't discuss conception.'

'You must have.'

'Well, we *didn't*.' She was angry now, too. 'You'll just have to take my word for it. He

165

asked something—said something about our waiting so long to have a baby and I guess my face...' She put her head down. 'Nobody but Max would have...'

'And of course you had been pregnant twice by him. He knew it had to be me.'

She stood up tiredly and took two steps towards him. 'I give up. I can't fight you any more, Arthur. I love you. Nothing as good as you ever happened to me. If you can't accept it, I don't know what I can do.'

He sat looking up at her, his face sagging with fatigue. For a long moment they were locked in a silent tableau. Then in a slow movement he raised his hand and reached for hers. 'All right, I believe you, Florence. I do. I *hate* it when there's trouble between us.' He was holding her hand so hard she caught her breath. 'I *hate* it. Let's try to forget all this. Max is dead. He won't ever bother us again.'

'Yes.' She met his eyes. 'He won't ever bother us again.' Something unspoken passed between them.

THURSDAY

CHAPTER EIGHTEEN

Tate went out early. Too early. The bell alongside Dawn's orange door brought no response. As he rang a second time, he

166

remembered that she walked by the water at this hour; he would have to return.

Driving up the road, he could see that someone was at home in the Bloch house; windows were open and Karin Bloch's car sat in the driveway. There was no sign of Marcie Terpstra. On an impulse he stopped. Keith Bloch and the two children were nowhere about. Karin answered the ring, a pot of glue in one hand.

'Oh, Detective Tate.' She did not sound precisely pleased.

'You're working.'

She recovered herself. 'No, no, it's all right. Come on in.'

'I will if you'll go on working. I'll just watch for a few minutes.'

She threw him a puzzled glance before she turned and led the way into her workroom. Walking behind her, he admired the rough blonde hair, the tall erect figure in its jeans and smock. This must be the sort of woman Scandinavian woodcarvers had used as their model for ship figureheads. He could imagine her with her hair blowing out behind her. When she glanced back at him, his face grew warm at his thoughts.

She was at work on some minute detail inside the building. He craned to see and then gave up. 'Tell me,' he said, 'why *do* people make miniatures?'

She laughed. 'They make such wonderful

conversation pieces, that's why. I don't know how many times I've been asked that. Do you know something? I'm going to let you in on a secret, something not many miniaturists admit.'

He could not tell whether she was serious or teasing. She read the question in his face. 'This is true. It's mastery.'

His face must have expressed his confusion. She went on. 'That's right. They must have lost control over their lives, maybe never had it. Or over their bodies in some way. But over their marvellous little miniatures they have perfect mastery. They've created a little world of their own where they do have control.'

'Ah. That explains it.'

'Only partially. I don't make miniatures for that reason—in fact, there are probably lots of miniaturists like me. For us, it's an exploration, I suppose. I love doing research, finding out exactly how a building would have been constructed, what sort of details would have been included. And now that I have a commission I feel productive, I'll be able to do other museum pieces. At first, I must say—' she stopped what she was doing and looked out of the window—'it was an escape. A sort of therapy.'

'You lost a child.'

She turned back to him. 'Yes, how did you know? Oh. The MADD meeting.'

'Yes. Is it something you can talk about?'

168

She straightened. 'It's hard, but I can. It was my first child, a girl. She was just a little older than Ricky. We were on the road, right out here, walking along the little footpath, way over to one side.' She raised her hands in a gesture that spoke her disbelief. 'She was ahead and this car—' she stopped to gain control of her voice—'this car came tearing up the hill at us. There was no time to move or think—or anything. He hit Janey.'

'Did he stop? Did you know who it was?'

'No, he veered and went around the corner and up that hill. He must have been drunk, he was all over the road. I didn't register anything—what the car looked like, the licence number, anything. All I could see was Janey...' She stopped. 'We never knew who did it.'

'It wasn't—it couldn't have been Max Follett?'

She turned towards her work, her back to him. 'I'm sure if it had been Max, he'd have stopped. He was never too drunk to have stopped. But I wouldn't let him in my house after that, not till he stopped drinking. I couldn't be ... reminded. So that's how I started working on miniatures. As a therapy of sorts.' She turned back to him. Her face was flushed with emotion.

'I'm so sorry.' It seemed inadequate beyond words. 'Actually,' he said, 'when I stopped by, all I meant to do was ask when Miss Terpstra gets back from her job. I need to see her.'

'She's back by one, unless they shop or stop off at the playground.'

'She manages well, doesn't she?' He wondered if the casual question fooled her. She was not easily fooled.

'Yes. I don't think I could do it. She's ingenious, does a lot with a little. I suppose there's a sort of challenge in that.'

'She writes, doesn't she?'

'A little, apparently. I never knew till this week. I did know she'd taken a fiction course with Max, but she said she'd dropped out.'

'She didn't consider him a good teacher?'

She looked at him as though she were perfectly following his line of questioning. She had possession of herself once more. 'Maybe too good. Critical. Very.'

'Her husband—I mean her young man— was a writer, too?'

'I don't know what he did. Not much, I gather. You'll have to ask her.'

'He did something. He made a baby.'

She did not respond.

'Were they together for a long time?'

'Not once he'd, as you put it, made a baby. He wanted no part of fatherhood.'

'Doesn't he even support the child?'

'Not a penny. The usual picture. He writes occasionally, tells her about himself, but—'

'Doesn't even ask about his son.'

'You have the picture. Now don't say

anything for a minute while I get this in place.'

He watched her, the light on her hair, her intent face with its faint flush, her upper body tilted towards the Victorian house. Suddenly he was aroused. What's happening to me? he thought. I'm coming to life again.

When she straightened she turned towards him. Her eyes were amused. 'I think you've pumped me about as much as I'll let myself be pumped. If you have more questions, I think it would be a good idea to ask *her*.'

'I didn't—' He stopped. 'Right. Don't stop what you're doing. I know the way out. Thanks for letting me watch. And ask.'

She leaned against the table, facing him. 'Any time, Detective.' Her eyes were mocking.

*　　　*　　　*

By the time he got to the bottom of the hill Dawn had returned from her walk. She was in the backyard, down on her knees in jeans, her feet bare. Nearby, the grey kitten chased something not visible to Tate.

'Planting?'

She looked up, unstartled, as though she had expected him. 'Not exactly. Weeding.' She eased to a standing position. 'My garden produces more weeds than vegetables. Hi. What's up?'

He felt as though he had known her for years. She was the reason for this . . . loosening he had felt all morning, this easing of the rigidity that had enclosed him for months. He wanted to hug her, not just for her, but for helping free him.

Instead he said, his voice sounding stiff to him, 'I need to talk to you about something important. Is there some place out back here where we can sit down?'

'Sure.' She led him to an L-shaped bench in the corner of the garden. 'Here we're perfectly private.'

'You look better today.'

'I feel better. I feel *good*.' She smiled widely. 'I have to buy some clothes today and I'm going to buy a dress, a real dress. And I think shoes with heels. And black stockings.' At his face, she laughed. 'You don't know what I'm talking about, do you? It's just that I haven't done anything like that for, oh, for *months*. I've decided it's all over, those things that have been happening to me. I think that's what the key meant, the key being returned. And I decided Max wouldn't want me to go on moping about the way I have. He'd want me to do something for myself, something to make me feel better. It makes me feel ... young to think of buying a dress.'

Tate had an almost irrepressible desire to put aside his role and say, 'I know, I know. All morning, Dawn...' He suppressed the impulse. 'I'm glad,' he said soberly. 'Now then.'

'Yes?'

'You know your brother left you his house, I gather.'

'Yes.'

'You didn't know anything about a will, though?'

'No.' After a moment she said, 'You found one.'

'Yes. You *were* left the house, free and clear. And ten thousand dollars.'

She said nothing. Muffin jumped into her lap.

'Did your brother have any children?'

She glanced down at the furry little creature. 'He had no children by any of his wives.'

'Or otherwise?'

'Otherwise? Would I know that?'

'You might.'

She lowered her head and contemplated her out-thrust toes. 'What are you getting at, Detective Tate?'

He sighed. 'Your brother left the bulk of his estate to Kevin Terpstra.'

She raised her head. 'Yes.'

'Yes? What does that mean?'

'It means Kevin was his son.'

'You knew?'

'Marcie didn't know I knew, but I did.'

'But how?' He reached out and took her arm as though to help brace her for what she was about to say.

'Max was twelve years older than I, so

173

naturally I never saw him as a little boy. But my parents had lots of pictures, and my mother had one on her dressing-table, taken when he was about four. Kevin looks just like that picture.' She shook her head. 'It's funny, I never really noticed it with Kevin himself. He's so active and with his blond colouring and seeing him with Marcie, it just never occurred to me. Then one day I was up in her apartment and I looked at that picture she has on her bookcase and I thought: Max—that's exactly like Mamma's picture. It seemed crazy then that I hadn't seen it all along.'

He removed his hand from her arm and they stared at each other. 'So that's what it reminded me of, that picture of Max,' he said. 'How did you feel?' he asked. It was not a policeman's question.

'I wondered if Max knew. As soon as I had that thought, I realized it was idiotic. Of course he knew. It explained why he'd become so interested in Marcie the last few weeks.'

'Did she ... were they ...?'

'No. I suppose it happened when she was up on campus. She took a class with him.'

'But you said he was interested in her.'

'I didn't say she was interested in him. She never said it to me, of course, but I think she disliked Max.'

'Your brother had a substantial estate, Dawn. Not huge, but larger than we anticipated. How do you feel about sharing the

174

larger portion with your nephew?'

She shrugged. 'I don't feel anything. They can use it. A house and ten thousand dollars is more than I've ever had.' She looked at him with mischief in her eyes. 'I can even buy an *expensive* dress now.' He realized she had never before let him see that she had humour in her make-up.

Tate found himself at a loss for further words. 'You'll hear about this more formally from the lawyer, I'm sure,' he said. 'Oh. One thing. Let us be the ones to tell Miss Terpstra, will you?' He stood up. 'Thanks, Dawn. I'm glad for you—about the house and money.'

She said nothing. When he let himself out of the crooked gate, she was sitting on the bench looking off into space, one hand on the kitten, her face wistful.

Missing her brother? Probably she'd rather have her only family back than this small wealth. But maybe, he reflected, she was just thinking about what that difference would mean. It must be strange to struggle along on a part-time job and suddenly come into a house and money, even a comparatively meagre sum like ten thousand dollars.

Then, as he pulled the car away from the kerb, an uneasy thought struck him. He hadn't said anything to her about not relaxing her guard, even if she did think the returned key had meaning. Then he shook off the notion. She had deadbolts and a chain now and she'd been warned about not leaving windows open. He couldn't very well treat her as though she were an infant. She was safe enough.

CHAPTER NINETEEN

Pedersen ran into no traffic and was there by 10.30.

It was the sort of town one passes through without realizing a town is there at all. On a whim, Pedersen parked his car on the corner of the main street behind a bus which had just pulled up. In lieu of a bus station, a Greyhound sign had been posted and a covered bench installed. Two people debarked, one a tiny white-haired man. Before the man could go on his way, Pedersen stopped him for directions. The town hall was three blocks from the corner on which he stood. Pedersen thanked the man, locked his car and strolled leisurely along the street.

From behind every window he sensed interest. A round-backed man kneeling in the hardware store window arranging garden tools looked up, his eyes sharp. From the other side of a plate glass window bearing a coffee-shop logo, heads swung towards him. An elderly waitress, tray in hand, walked to the window and looked him over without embarrassment. Two grey-haired women walking in his direction ducked glances at him, careful not to stare, and moved closer to each other. He smiled at another passing matron and was met by a steely glare.

On the opposite side of the street, a little unpainted shingle house with a short flight of rickety steps bore a hand-lettered sign: Public Library. Probably the volunteer effort of some booklover kept it going. He wondered if a citizen had willed a personal library to the town; often in villages such as this that was the inception of a public book collection. He was tempted to enter right then to see what the townspeople read. Maybe later. Tate would not have postponed a visit to the place.

The town hall was a small brick building with a plaque indicating its birthdate in the century before. He climbed the steps that led inside and entered. A clerk whose slightly goiterish gaze gave her a startled appearance looked up from the newspaper she was reading. The unfamiliar face brought her to attention.

Pedersen made his smile as engaging as possible. 'Good afternoon. I wonder if you can give me some help.' He opened his identification folder.

Her response was uneasy. 'Police? From Bay Cove?'

'I'm investigating a possible murder. I'm sure you've heard of the death of Mr Follett.'

Comprehension flooded her bony little face. 'Oh. Wasn't that terrible? But—was it—was he

177

murdered?'

'We're operating under that assumption. What I'm particularly interested in are records you may have—marriage records, records of birth, any criminal records.'

'Criminal?' She was shocked. 'I'm sure there weren't any criminal records. Besides, the police would have those.'

Pedersen had wanted her reaction towards the suggestion of anything untoward. 'Of course. Mr Follett's sister says her parents were married before the Second World War, 'thirty-seven or 'thirty-eight. And I'd like to glance at the records of birth—Doris Follett is thirty-six, that's 'fifty-two. Her brother was nineteen-forty.'

Three-quarters of an hour later, he emerged, not much wiser. Emmeline Black, aged 20, had married Irwin Follett, aged 23, in 1937. Three years later she had borne a son, Maxim, and twelve years after that a daughter, Doris.

The death certificates completed the picture. Irwin Follett had been born in 1914 in Rochester, New York, his parents in Poland. He had died in 1967 of a coronary thrombosis. His primary occupation was listed as salesman of medical products. Emmeline Black had entered the world in 1917 in Buffalo, New York, her parents born in the United States. She had been a housewife. She had died in 1974 of stomach cancer. He left the building. Except for the niggling thought that Black was not far

178

afield from Bloch, he had learned nothing worth mulling over, and that was probably coincidence.

'If you want information, try the drugstore,' the clerk called after him.

Down the street, the police records offered nothing at all. The ancient clerk—no police were in evidence—shook his head vigorously. 'Not the Folletts. Respectable folk. Had a fire out their place one time. Nothing serious. But criminal? No sirree.' The records bore him out, but Pedersen lingered. 'Did you know the family?'

'Not so's you'd say know. Said 'mornin' if we ran into one another.'

'Mr Follett was never drafted?'

'Nope. He had a kid. And those eyes of his.' He grinned wickedly. 'Wore thick glasses. Like the bottom of a water tumbler. Real Four-Eyes.' With a bony finger he complacently settled his own, thinner-lensed spectacles.

'Does the town have a hospital?'

'*This* town? The nearest's up at Cruden Springs. That's where the babies get born. There's a wing for the mental ones, too. Some end up there.'

Pedersen moved to another topic. 'You knew Max Follett had become quite famous for that book of his?'

'Sure did. We had these reporter fellows all over the place one year, taking pictures of us.' He beamed amusement. 'Interesting

179

characters, that's what we were. They liked the chief to stand out there by his patrol car, lean on it. When Matt, he's the druggist, heard they were coming, he changed his whole window, got all these old apo—apoc—' He gave up.

'Apothecary jars?'

'That's it. And big jars with coloured water. Still has 'em in his window. Visitors think we're—what'd that one lady say?—quaint. Quaint!' He snorted. 'Now my grandmother, she was quaint.'

Pedersen smiled. 'I'll have to drop by that store. What's the druggist's name again?'

'Matt Haycraft. Past retirement age, but I don't think he'll ever sell the place. Maybe he can get his son back here to take it.' He looked at Pedersen closely. 'You're a detective, you say?'

'Yes. I showed you my badge, remember?'

'The chief'll be here after dinner. He'll want to meet you if you're going to be around a while. Chief Wilson.'

'I'll try to get back, but I'm heading out for Bay Cove again this afternoon. Who would you suggest I talk to who might have really known the Folletts? It's a long time, I know.'

'Maybe the Daisches, they lived next door. Ask Matt. He'd know somebody. He knows this town inside out.'

On the pavement again, Pedersen was aware of the oppressive warmth. The morning had been warm but a slight breeze had blown; now the air did not stir. The familiar chill, faint but so often present in the air of Bay Cove at this hour, did not exist in the land-locked town. Heat did not agree with him.

Matt Haycraft's pharmacy and ice-cream parlour did exude an air of quaintness, from the handsome blue and white ceramic jars in the window to the white wire chairs at the three small marble-topped tables. At the moment the store was empty of customers except for a single teenager examining a rack of paperbacks.

'Couple of new science-fiction there, Jimmy,' Haycraft called as Pedersen entered. He turned to the detective, his manner only mildly curious. 'Can I get something for you, sir?' He was as tall as Pedersen, level-eyed, with a faint bloom on his cheek suggestive of high blood pressure.

Pedersen opened his badge-holder. 'I'm here in connection with Max Follett's death. The consensus seems to be that you're the one to help me.'

Haycraft looked doubtful. 'Help you with what?'

Pedersen looked around. The heat and the long drive had suddenly caught up with him; his eyelids were heavy. 'Do you serve coffee at your soda-fountain? Maybe I could have a cup and we could talk.'

The coffee was strong. The boy selected a book and left. Alone in the store, Pedersen and

181

Haycraft faced each other across one of the small tables, each eyeing the other with interest. 'Now what was I supposed to help with?' Haycraft asked.

Pedersen smiled. 'Actually, I'm not sure you can. I'm investigating a death—actually a murder, we're pretty sure. Did you know Max Follett?'

Haycraft's expression changed subtly. 'I did.' He volunteered nothing.

'And the parents, I suppose? And Doris?'

'I knew them. The Folletts, the parents, weren't sociable people, my wife and I never visited back and forth with them. Their only close friends were the Daisches. They're just back from their daughter's in Arizona. What did you want to know about the Folletts?'

Pedersen settled more firmly on the unsteady wire-legged chair. 'Were they liked in the community? Was there any scandal? Any intrigue you know of?' Before the other man could speak, he raised a hand. 'I'm sure you don't deal in gossip, not habitually, but this is a murder, Mr Haycraft, and it may have its roots back here.' He grinned. 'It may not, of course, too. I may be all wrong. But, since you asked, that is what I'm trying to find out.'

Haycraft's face was puzzled. 'I never heard anything. No rumours, nothing. And in a place the size of Longville you hear rumours if there's anything to hear. They seemed perfectly respectable. He didn't have a mistress. She didn't have a lover.' He laughed. 'Even the idea seems crazy. If they did, they kept the fact well hidden.'

'What about business dealings? Property? Any struggles in those areas?'

Haycraft shrugged. 'What business? He sold medical supplies for some big house in Sacramento. Visited doctors with samples, took orders from places like mine. All on a pretty small scale. They made out all right, but I doubt they put by a lot. And the only property I know of they owned was their house.'

'Where was their house? I'd like to walk by. Pick up a sense of the ambience.'

Haycraft frowned. 'Around on Jerrold. Twenty-seven. It's just a few blocks.' He laughed suddenly, open-mouthed, easy. 'In Longville *everything's* just a few blocks. Except the canning factory. That's a couple of miles out.'

'And the Daisches? The best friends?'

'They're pleasant folks.' He rose to help a customer. 'How are you, Mrs Stein? What can I do for you?'

Mrs Stein pondered rather longer than Pedersen thought necessary over the purchase of a box of Band-Aids and a jar of Pond's Cold Cream; then, obviously miffed that she was not to have the stranger in town explained or introduced, took herself off, her step brisk. Haycraft remained behind the counter.

Pedersen picked up his cup and strolled over. 'You did know Max Follett, you said. And his sister.'

'The sister, no. She came in for a cone or a soda sometimes, quiet little thing, cute-looking, but I never talked with her. Max was different. He liked an audience. He had all sorts of ideas, ideas about everything, and he tried them out on anybody who'd hold still. He was bright, too, he and a couple of his pals. The three of them worked on the school paper and I think they all thought they'd be writers when they finished college. One of Max's friends, Billy Fitzgerald, is a writer—he works on a news magazine now. The other one, Tom Whitaker, went to Iowa where they have some sort of programme for writers. But he went on to be a teacher. Professor. North Carolina, I think. They'd come by, buy a Coke apiece and sit there tossing their ideas around. Cocky, but bright. I enjoyed it. It was a change from all the biddies looking for a new lipstick colour.'

'Max Follett dropped in on you about ten years ago, didn't he?'

Haycraft's eyebrows shot up. 'How'd you know that? He did, it was right around the time that book of his was published. Had his wife, little blonde woman, with him. He was all upset they'd changed his old house, taken off the porch. And he wanted to hear what I knew of Tom and Billy. You'd think they'd have been in touch with him after that book came out.'

'Maybe they were. I understand Follett was drinking heavily then, maybe he wasn't aware of who was in touch and who wasn't.'

'That was it, then. I thought they must have been partying, celebrating the book. He smelled of liquor that day he came in.'

'He joined AA later. Divorced his wife, but got back to his typewriter.'

'Poor Max. Too bad about him. Mustn't have been out of his forties, and the paper said a new book was coming out.'

'It is too bad. It's especially too bad if it's murder.'

'Well—' Haycraft picked up an order book—'I wouldn't know about that. You talk to the Daisches. Want to phone them you're coming? You can use my phone back here.'

When Pedersen returned, Haycraft said, 'You know where to go? Larchmont—second corner to the right, then turn left. It's forty-two. And you needn't warn me not to say anything. I don't talk.' He chuckled. 'Not often, that is. No.' He waved Pedersen's hand away. 'The coffee's on the house. In memory of Max. I can see him there now, over at the fountain, skinny, with all that wild hair, talking so hard he almost fell off the stool.' He pursed his lips. 'The coffee's in memory of Max and all those ideas of his.'

CHAPTER TWENTY

Given the time since his phone call to them, it was surprising: the Daisches had managed to prepare for his visit as if it were a special occasion. A table in the living-room had been spread with a cloth and on it had been placed one handsome blue-patterned plate holding slices of golden pound cake and another heaped with cookies, discernibly homemade. These kept company with a highly polished silver creamer and sugar bowl and three blue-patterned cups and saucers. The teaspoons and forks gleamed. As Mr Daisches accompanied Pedersen into the room, his wife entered from another door, carrying a silver coffee-server. Their movements seemed choreographed; they gave the impression of having worked out such details to perfection.

The room was suspiciously immaculate, as though the furnishings had been set in place years before and the room seldom entered since except for periodic ritual cleanings. The light wood, the blue and green fabric on the sofa, part of a three-piece suite, spoke of the 'forties. When he was a child, Pedersen's mother had bought a chair very like the one he was being offered; he remembered her talking to his father at dinner of the daring new colour combination. Pedersen took for granted there was some other room, perhaps once called the 'rec room', now the 'family room', in which they put up their feet and relaxed, read, talked, watched television, actually lived.

'You must be tired after your long trip,' he said. 'I understand you've been visiting family in Arizona. Isn't it hot there at this time of the year?'

'We never moved away from the air-conditioning,' Mrs Daisches confided. 'I don't know how people there *lived* before air-conditioning.'

'I never feel jet-lag till the second day,' Mr Daisches contributed. 'The first day I feel unnaturally awake. Odd, isn't it?'

Pedersen smiled. 'It's generous of you to give me time.'

'We want to help,' said Mrs Daisches. Her face was earnest.

'Yes,' said Mr Daisches. He sounded less sure. 'We don't know exactly how you want us to help, though.'

'As I said when I phoned, it's your old friends, the Folletts. I understand you were their next-door neighbours and closest friends.'

They nodded.

'You know Max Follett was found dead, electrocuted. There was evidence that it was not an accident. We are quite sure from consequent events that it was intentional.'

'Not *suicide*?' Mrs Daisches asked,

187

disbelieving.

'No. Murder.'

'What kind of consequent events?' Mr Daisches asked.

'There have been a couple of attacks—purely symbolic, so far, she's all right—on Dawn. Sorry, Doris. She uses the name Dawn these days.'

'What a funny thing to do,' said Mrs Daisches. She did not seem to be following the essential part of the story.

'We had thought,' Pedersen said, 'that it might be not just Max who was the intended victim, but the *family*—what's left of it.'

'You mean Doris might be killed, too?' Her eyes were wide.

'We're certainly trying to prevent that. But someone appears to be trying to tell her something.'

'I still don't quite see,' said Mr Daisches, 'where we come in. Did you want her to come stay with us?'

'No, no, she'd never—she'd appreciate your offer, I'm sure, but she has a job in Bay Cove. And her other work. She's a potter.' He accepted another slice of pound cake. 'Your own? It's delicious.'

Mrs Daisches ducked her head.

'No, my feeling was that there may have been enmity. Some grudge, perhaps, that had been directed against all four of the Folletts. Something that originated way back. There

188

seems to be no other reason for both Max and Doris being under attack, the other connections are too loose. She was not involved in Max's work in any way and he wasn't in hers. Even their friends were different. She hadn't achieved any celebrity, nothing anyone could have envied or resented.'

'I see,' said Mr Daisches. It was clear he didn't.

'I came to you hoping you'd tell me more about the family. From everything I've learned, you knew them best.'

They looked at each other. He spoke first. 'They were just ordinary people. Neighbourly, with us at least. Went to church. Kept their lawn mowed. Their kids were polite, did well in school.'

'Were they—this is hard to ask, I know you don't want to gossip—but were they people who would have confided in you if there had been anything?'

Mrs Daisches spoke. 'Emmie and I were pretty tight; we spent a lot of time together. I guess she'd have told me.'

'Perhaps what I'm looking for has to do with the children. You knew them well?'

'Well now, you know Max was older. They were more like two little families, first one with Max, then one with Doris.' She smiled. 'I knew Doris better. She was the same age as one of my girls. But I heard about Max. They were awfully proud of him.'

'They thought the earth revolved around him,' Mr Daisches put in.

'He was talented even as a boy?'

'Yes. Always winning prizes. Of course he was an only child for twelve years. She had—' she glanced at her husband and went on—'another pregnancy and almost died. Once the doctor told her not to try again, she just ... focused on Max.'

'That must have been hard on him.'

She looked surprised. 'Hard? Why?'

'I just mean that kids do better with a little ... benign neglect, don't you think? Being focused on is a big responsibility.'

Mr Daisches spoke. 'He was a spoiled kid. My wife never saw it, but he was arrogant. I hate arrogance in kids.'

Pedersen smiled. 'His friends say he was a difficult man, too.'

Mrs Daisches did not like their being the source of unflattering opinions. 'Now,' she said, her tone placating, 'you know, dear, we never knew him. Not the way we knew Doris.'

Pedersen put down his cup and settled more comfortably into his chair. 'Tell me about her. Any boyfriends her family objected to, anything like that?'

'Well now—' this seemed a favourite warm-up to the expression of Mrs Daisches's ideas—'she was a sweet little thing. Pretty. And bright as a button.'

'Once she came along, *she* was her parents'
190

pet, I hear.'

Mr and Mrs Daisches exchanged glances. 'I wouldn't say that,' she said starchily. 'Emmie and Irv were *fair*. They treated the children exactly the same.'

'No favouritism? Cute little girl born after Mrs Follett had all but given up on another child?'

'She *had* given up,' said Mrs Daisches.

'What my wife means is that she wasn't pleased when she learned she was going to have another.'

'Well now, Emil, she was scared. Remember what her doctor had told her.'

'I thought it was more than that.'

She cut him off. 'Emil, you don't know. Emmie and I talked a lot. She was pleased to have a daughter. Every mother wants at least one daughter.'

'I suppose so,' Mr Daisches grudgingly agreed. 'She didn't treat either of her kids the way you did ours.'

'He means the way I'd hug and tease and kiss our girls—You know the way you do. Emmie was different, she just couldn't be— demonstrative, I guess you'd call it. It didn't mean she didn't love them. Emmie told me things—I know. It was too bad they couldn't show it, but I'm sure the children knew, children know these things. And—' she looked at her husband with admonishment—'they were fair. They even built a beautiful little gazebo for her. They'd built a treehouse for Max when he was little and then the gazebo for her. I think Max was pleased for her, too. You know, she adored him. He was awfully good to her for a brother who was so much older. He could just have treated her as a little pest, the way some big brothers do.'

'I must say that's true,' her husband said. 'He was good. Especially when she was hurt that time.'

'Hurt?' Pedersen sat forward a little, aware that at last he had come closer to the answer he was seeking.

'Well now...' Mrs Daisches began.

CHAPTER TWENTY-ONE

The meetings were always called for 1.30. At 1.45 Leona, in flat sandals and a blue-flowered cotton dress that did good things for her eyes, strolled down the road towards the Bloch house. Keith was not working in the yard, and there was no sign of Marcie or her little boy out back. She approached the side door, which faced away from the Smith house, and rang, prepared, should Florence or Marcie appear, with explanations, forgotten details for Karin to have carried to the meeting. No neighbour appeared, nor did Keith. She rang again, listening to the sound echo through the empty house, almost, it seemed, through an empty neighbourhood. Apparently Keith was doing the errands without Karin.

She turned, so angry she was close to tears, and climbed the long hill back to her house. At 2.0, impatient with pretending to work, she phoned. Still no one there. It seemed impossible that all her planning was to come to nothing. Leona had long since learned that with proper attention to detail, she could make most things happen as she wished. Today appeared to be an exception. A second call at 2.15 went unanswered. At 2.45 she made one final try. This time the phone was picked up. It was now too late: the children would be arriving home and, shortly, Karin too.

With an effort she made her tone jaunty. 'Keith? Karin back yet? She was filling in for me at a meeting.'

'I know, she left a note. She says she'll be in by four. Is there a message?'

She hesitated. 'No.' She kept her voice light. 'What's happening with you? I sort of expected you'd stroll up one afternoon or evening.'

His silence told her he was thinking that over. 'We've been busy. Up to our ears, both of us.'

'I wasn't speaking of both of you, Keith. Just you.'

His laugh was uncomfortable. 'Papers. Lecture notes. You know.'

Clearly, this was not going to be worked out by phone; it needed her presence. Max had once called her face flowerlike. Pure, he had said. She knew how men responded to her appearance and she had long since given up resenting the fact that often it was only to her appearance that they responded. It's me, she had told herself, what they find in my face is me. Why should I feel there is some shame in being beautiful? In making men want me?

Impulsively she glanced at her diary and said, 'Keith, I'd like you two to come to dinner. Would tomorrow night do? I'll ask Marcie. And Dawn too—we should do something to take her out of herself. And I'll want to hear about today's meeting.'

The return to normalcy in the conversation was met by open relief. 'Sounds fine. We don't have a thing on the diary for tomorrow. I'll talk to Karin when she comes in. She'll get back to you.'

Not even a thank-you. She had better wait until she heard from Karin before asking the others. She put down the phone conscious of an irritability such as she had not known in a long time. Perhaps she was making a mistake with Keith. But she needed someone. Someone strong. Putting all that happened in the past week out of her mind was not enough. She could push aside the events but the sense of isolation persisted. Perhaps a dinner-party would help in more ways than one. Meanwhile she had another evening to get through. She picked up the phone again. Maybe Perry could be coaxed to join her for dinner at the new Vietnamese place. Perry was alone, too.

* * *

It was after four before Tate reached Marcie Terpstra, just as he was about to give up on her for the day.

She seemed surprised that anyone had been aware of her absence. 'You've been trying to get me? Kevin and I went to a Day Care picnic. We've been swimming and building sand castles and stuffing ourselves with franks.' She sounded relaxed and merry.

'Could we talk for a few minutes, Miss Terpstra? I could come by right now.' Tate reflected that these days he was in that neighbourhood as much as his own.

'Well ... Kevin would be around. My attention would be pretty divided. I—' she hesitated—'I don't suppose later is at all possible? He goes to bed at seven.'

Tate amended his plans for the early evening. 'That should work. Why don't you give me a call after your son gets to sleep?' He gave her the number. Hanging up, he reminded himself that he was too young to be looking forward to an evening before TV with a beer and his feet up. Being divorced had in some subtle way eroded his youth. Maybe a little evening work would be stimulating. He might even stop afterwards at a bar he liked, that quasi-Irish place, sit around a while and listen to some music. Aside from all that, he'd like presenting Pedersen with at least some indications of effort.

She phoned before seven. He had gone out for a hamburger and returned to his office, where he was sitting over paperwork.

'Kevin couldn't keep his eyes open. He's *out*. It's safe to come.'

'Fine. Give me fifteen minutes.' Once again he was struck by what a cooperative bunch this was. He and Pedersen had reflected less flatteringly on them at the beginning, but the impression he now had was that they were all extending themselves in the effort to help. He wondered if she would be so agreeable when she learned his errand: whatever her reason, she had made it a point not to reveal her relationship with Max Follett. It could be that she did not realize her child was Max's and not her young man's. If Dawn's testimony as to the photographs had been accurate, as well as the little tug of recognition on his own part when he had seen Max's photograph as a little boy, and if Max's wishes had been properly interpreted, the evidence was strong that Kevin was indeed Max's child.

He found her sitting out on a little patio behind her house. She looked pink from the sun and cheerful. 'I waited with my dessert. If you don't want any ice-cream, you'll just have to watch me eat it.' She indicated a chair. 'Isn't

196

this great? It's Keith—he loves doing things for people. He put in the bricks and built the sandbox for Kevin, and I did the potted plants. Pretty grand for a garage apartment.' She left him sitting amid the pots of pink geraniums and blue lobelia and went off upstairs for ice-cream.

They finished eating it before they talked. Setting his empty bowl on the little table beside him, Tate said, 'That hit the spot. Now. What I have to tell you may come as a large surprise. First, though, I have to ask you a question.'

Apprehension brushed her face.

For some reason, probably his sudden sense of her vulnerability, he found it hard to ask. 'It's about Kevin's father.'

'What about his father?' Her face told him she knew what was coming.

'Is Max Follett Kevin's father?'

She grew still. 'Now why would you think that?'

'Marcie—may I call you that?—I think you should just tell me.'

'First you tell me why you think that.'

'We've had access to his will.'

She sat straight up. 'You mean he left something to Kevin?'

'Yes.'

'Well.' Her eyes met his. 'I never expected *that*.' She sat studying the geraniums. Finally she sighed and said, 'Max was his father.' She laughed shortly. 'I've just sworn Perry to

197

secrecy about it.'

'Excuse me for having to ask this, but are you sure? You were living with someone, I understand.' As soon as he asked, he realized it was only curiosity that had fuelled the question. The will, the inheritance, perhaps even her motives, were in no way altered by his knowing the answer.

She appeared unaware that it was an inappropriate question. 'We were together, you might say, in name only. The man I was living with was pretty heavily into drugs. The last thing on his mind was sex. Around the time Kevin was conceived, I had only one—' her eyebrows went up—'sexual contact, I guess you'd call it. One of those one-time mistakes you read about in novels that always end up in the conception of a child.' She smiled at him. 'My mother always warned me.'

'Your husband—I mean, your housemate— knew it wasn't his, then?'

'Yes.' She shrugged. 'It gave him a good excuse for leaving. I should add that I was glad to see him go, though I'd have liked a daddy for Kevin. Not that one, though.'

'You and Max Follett didn't consider marrying?'

'I never told him about the baby being his. It's just in the last few months that it seems to have dawned on him that it could be his child. Lately he's been after me to marry him, all but blackmailing me into it. He had no other kids

198

and I guess now that he was older he wanted someone to carry on—' she frowned—'the line.'

'I don't understand. How could he blackmail you?'

'He threatened to take Kevin away from me, make me out to be an unfit mother, depriving Kevin of the life that he could have as Max's son. He seemed to think he could prove Kevin was his. You can't do that, can you? I was told you can only prove whose child it *isn't*. It scared me, all the same. And I didn't want him around, trying to bribe me, buy me, seduce me—something—all the time.'

'So you must have been quite ambivalent when you learned Follett was dead?'

'I certainly didn't feel any sense of personal loss. I didn't, however—' she looked at him levelly—'hurry him on his way, if that's what you're implying.'

'I'm not implying anything. At any rate, Mr Follett's will should make life easier for you. If you want to bring your son up as he would have been brought up as Max Follett's son, you should be able to now.'

She stood up. 'That never was an aspiration of mine. I should go up and check to be sure Kevin is OK. Are there going to be any other questions?'

'No. Yes, one. I wonder why you went to that party for Follett.'

'Party? Oh, at Leona's. I didn't want to call

attention to our ... situation. I figured the more casual I was with Max, the better. From everybody's point of view, including his. If I'd seemed threatened, then he'd have really moved in. I treated the whole thing as nonsense, as a figment of his exhausted brain. Anything else?'

'Not for now. You're probably as tired as Kevin after your day in the sun. I'll go along.'

As he walked down the drive, the thought skittered across his mind that perhaps Max *had* moved in, despite her casual handling of the matter.

Getting back into the car, he speculated on stopping at the Irish pub. It seemed less appealing than it had an hour ago and not much fun alone. No, he thought as he pulled the car out of the driveway and into the road, I'll just get along home and mull a little over this case. Or, he added to himself as he passed the house with the orange door, watch a little TV.

FRIDAY

CHAPTER TWENTY-TWO

Pedersen had barely entered the office when Dawn's call came. She was crying. 'Detective Pedersen, I think you'd better come up.'

'Dawn, what is it? Have you been hurt?'

'No, not me. It's my—Muffin. Can you come? Or Detective Tate?'

They both went. As though she had given up on all caution, she had left both the front door and the door to her apartment open. She was huddled in a corner of the sofa-bed, a soggy handkerchief pressed to her face. 'There.' She pointed and looked away. Lying on the worktable under a newspaper was Muffin, now a flat bundle of wet fur. 'She was in my bathtub.' She shuddered. 'I'll never be able to take a bath there again.'

'When did it happen?'

'I don't know. It was like the last time. I went for my walk and came back and found—that.' She lifted her eyes to Tate's. 'It's going to be me next.'

'Dawn!' Tate said. 'You simply have to get out of here. This stubbornness of yours *will* get you hurt. Now think. Where can you go?'

'He's right, Dawn,' Pedersen said.

'I'm not going anywhere. I'm staying here. I need the kiln, I need my clay—I'm just not going anywhere.'

'Can't you get someone to come and stay with you?'

'Who? And where would they stay? This apartment isn't big enough for me, much less for someone else.'

Tate looked at Pedersen. 'She could stay at her brother's. They've finished with the house. There's more room there.'

201

Dawn stuffed the wet handkerchief into her pocket in a brisk gesture. 'I'm not going anyplace. I'll go up this weekend and go through Max's things and later on I may move up there, but I don't want anyone with me. I couldn't work with someone around. I'll be all right. Or I won't. I'm sure whatever's going to happen will happen no matter how many people live with me.'

Tate raised his voice. 'Don't you care if you live or die?'

'I care.' She looked at his angry face and said gently. 'And thank you for caring. You're both nice men.'

'Did you have your chain on the door?' asked Pedersen. 'Oh no, you'd just been out.'

'Somebody has a key, that's all.'

Pedersen nodded. 'It looks that way. You had more than one key to the deadbolt?'

'Don't ask. I don't know where it is.'

Tate snorted. 'Then let's change the lock again. This time *we'll* keep the extra key.' He looked at her closely. 'Let me ask you again, Dawn. Is there anyone who would have a *reason* to be doing these things? Anyone here? Anyone you knew earlier? Anyone your brother knew?'

She shook her head impatiently. 'I told you before. I don't know why someone has it in for me. I can't think of a thing. Do you suppose they're messages for me?'

'If they are, the sender's covered just about

everything by now.' He glanced at her jeans, stiff with newness. 'I see you've bought some new clothes.'

'A couple of things. Nothing much.' She looked at Tate. 'I bought the dress, then I had a dinner invitation to go with it. If it weren't for—'

'I know. It casts a pall over everything.'

'Two deaths...' she said.

'Let's send for the locksmith,' Pedersen said.

* * *

'I'm even beginning to suspect him,' Dawn said, after the man had tested the new lock, received her cheque and closed the gate. She sounded tired, defeated.

'Don't worry about the locksmith. Now you keep that key with you, around your neck on a ribbon or something, so no one can get at it.' Pedersen pocketed the second key. 'We'll take charge of this one.'

'I do feel safer. I guess we should have thought of this when Max's key was returned and my clothes were cut.'

'We should,' Pedersen said. 'Now, Dawn, be careful. If you have to go somewhere at night, give us a ring. We'll send a car up for you.'

She frowned. 'I can lock my car. You're making a prisoner of me.'

'Please, Dawn.'

'Oh, all right. If somebody doesn't offer to

203

come and pick me up. Thank you, I feel better.'
She glanced at the newspaper-covered hump
on the worktable.

'I'll stay and help you bury Muffin,' Tate
said, not looking at Pedersen.

'We'll both help,' said Pedersen. Police work
included a lot of variety these days.

*   *   *

'Well,' Tate said, as they pulled away from
Dawn's house, 'was it worth it, the Longville
trip? Find out anything?'

'I found out a lot. Before I tell you, I want
you to give Harner a ring, try him again.' They
rounded the corner and headed down to town.

'Dawn's husband? I thought he said he
didn't know anything.'

'I know. I think he's been holding out on us.
Or maybe he doesn't realize that what he hasn't
mentioned is important. If I tell you what I
learned in Longville, you'll be tempted to lead
him.'

Tate threw a puzzled glance his way. 'I'm
quite able to—oh well, let's do it your way.'

*   *   *

Back at headquarters, Pedersen found what he
had been waiting for. Lying on his desk was a
fat envelope with the banners of colour that
proclaimed Express Mail.

204

Tate indicated the envelope. 'Is that what I think it is?'

'Yes. When I called, they'd just received the manuscript themselves. Considering that, they're right on the ball.'

'You're hoping it'll give you a few clues?'

'Maybe, depending on how autobiographical it is. It may give me some ideas on the Folletts' family life.'

'Usually it's first books that are autobiographical. You going to start on it now?'

'I'd like to. Ron, why don't you try Harner now? Let him ramble, if that's what it takes, tell you everything he thinks of.'

*   *   *

It took several calls. Harner was at lunch, he was in conference, he had just stepped out of the office. Was the caller sure he didn't want Mr Harner to phone back?

Finally, Tate hit the right moment.

'Mr Harner, Detective Tate. You're a hard man to pin down.'

'Oh, it's you. I have a few minutes now. What's up?'

'What's up is that we're puzzled. We told you Dawn was fine, we didn't want to worry you unnecessarily, but a couple of things have happened that have made us wonder if she is fine.'

205

There was a short silence. 'She hasn't been hurt?'

'No, not yet, but—let me ask you the question that's on my mind. Is there anything, anything at all, that you recall her mentioning that might explain why both she and her brother are under attack?'

'You asked me that before. I should think the best source of information would be Doris herself.' He paused. 'What sort of attack?'

'Her cat Muffin was drowned. That's coming very close. You see, we thought at first maybe these attacks—the gazebo she had worked on for the museum show was destroyed, her clothing was slashed and her pottery mutilated—came *because* she was Follett's sister. It's beginning to look as though there's nothing symbolic about these—gestures. They look very real. And they're directed against her. At her, I mean.'

'My God, that sounds serious. Isn't there some way to protect her? Send her away or give her twenty-four-hour police protection?'

'She's upset, but she refuses to go anywhere else or have anyone move in with her. And we're giving her what police protection we can. Let's get back to my question. Think. What do you know about her childhood, her family?'

'You've asked her this?'

'Yes. Either she can't or—' he had had a sudden sense of disloyalty—'won't tell us.'

'I don't know anything. That is, I know she

206

was born when her brother was practically a teenager. Her mother had some trouble and wasn't supposed to have more kids. Doris was unplanned.'

This was better. 'Her parents must have been pleased, though,' Tate interjected conversationally.

'I would have thought so, but they sounded like a pretty undemonstrative pair. Hovering, demanding, but—cold.'

'They built her a gazebo, I understand.'

'Yes, and they built Max a treehouse when he was little. I think they prided themselves on being even-handed. It's just that they sounded ... cold, like cold people. And very hard on the kids. Expected them to be perfect. Criticized everything they did. It was hell on Doris's self-esteem, let me tell you. I guess both kids were bright and couldn't help achieving—that was just fortunate for them.'

'The gazebo was all hers?'

'It was till it burned down.'

Tate sat up. 'Burned down?'

'Oh, hasn't Doris told you? That's why she was so crazy about Max—he saved her life.'

Tate said, 'Maybe you'd better begin at the beginning.'

'It was the summer she was eight, I think. Max had come home from college to do some writing—he was writing even then. One evening the parents went to some church function and left Doris in his care. He was up in

207

his room, writing, it was getting on towards dusk and apparently Doris decided to take a candle from the sideboard where they were stored and light the gazebo with it. The place caught fire. She was burned.'

Tate could guess. 'Her legs?'

'Yes. Not badly, but her legs were slightly scarred. The important thing is that Max looked out of the window at the right moment or something. He got her out of the gazebo in time. She could have burned to death. I guess it scared the hell out of him—after all, he was supposed to be taking care of her. He even refused to go back to college until she was out of the hospital. After that, she adored him.'

'If her parents were cold people, perhaps he seemed more like a real parent to her.'

'Maybe. Undemonstrativeness wasn't his problem.' His tone was dry.

'No, but the man takes on new dimensions the more I learn of him.' Tate was silent for a moment. 'You know, this is interesting, like a piece of a puzzle, but it doesn't explain why someone should be persecuting Dawn.'

'I know. I told you I couldn't help. But it's the only major event in her life that I know about. And she wasn't even badly burned. She's just self-conscious. Probably those parents of hers. She's not *perfect* now.'

'Nothing else about the parents?'

'They sounded like pretty conventional people. Her mother stayed home and baked,

208

sewed Doris's clothes. She checked her homework every night. The father was the breadwinner.'

'And they're both long since dead.'

'Yes. Buried in Longville, where she lived.'

'We'll have to mull this over. But I'd like you to do the same. If you think of anything else, would you let me know?'

'I will, but what about Doris? You're going to *do* something, aren't you?'

'We'll do what we can. We'll keep an eye on her.' He looked sadly at the receiver. 'That's all we can do.'

*   *   *

Tate broke in on Pedersen's reading. 'Sorry, I know you're trying to make headway with that.'

'Did you learn anything?'

'I learned the source of her strong attachment to her brother. He saved her life when she was a kid. She set fire to her gazebo fooling around with candles and he got her out.'

'Her legs were burned?'

'Yes. I thought of it right away, too. The coloured stockings. It can't be much, though; Harner never even mentioned it the first time we spoke to him. He says she's not badly scarred.'

'But she's self-conscious about it. That's

why she didn't tell us herself. I wonder if that's what she meant when she said she was being sent messages'.

'What do you mean?'

'I mean someone here in town knows about the gazebo incident and is using it to threaten her.'

'What about the other things—the clothes and the kitten?'

'Underlining. Destruction headed your way. I think the crushing of the gazebo was the big message: the next thing may be fire.'

'*Arson?*'

'Yes. The question is, what's she doing that anyone would want to threaten her?'

'But who would know? The way she keeps her legs covered, it doesn't seem like something she'd have talked about.'

'Not in general conversation. She could have confided in someone.'

'God! And this Muffin business, too. Just when she was beginning to feel better.'

Pedersen looked at him.

'I mean, she looked so exhausted the first few times I saw her and she was sleeping terribly. But when I went over yesterday to talk about the will, she seemed better, as though she were shaking it off and pulling herself together.' He sighed. 'Do you find it possible to connect anyone in this crowd with an idea like arson?'

'No, I admit I don't. They're a singularly . . . agreeable bunch.' Their eyes met. 'Agreeable

210

people can be murderers.'

Tate indicated the manuscript. 'You finding anything?'

'I've had a lot of interruptions. I don't mean you, other things. I'm going to get down to it now.' He removed the cover sheet from the manuscript.

But he had trouble getting down to it.

*　　*　　*

He and Freda had sat over dinner late the evening before, talking. The conversation had disturbed him.

Things had returned to normal between them. 'You've tuned in again,' she announced as they sat over their second cups of coffee.

'I have? I wasn't aware I'd tuned out.'

'You had. But you're listening to me again. I can see why you didn't, Carl, it's pretty discouraging.' She picked up her coffee-cup. 'What's happening with the case?'

'I'm not sure anything is. If I could work full time on it, but even then ... Ron's been doing a lot. Talking to the neighbours, checking details.'

'You think one of the neighbours did it?'

'I do, but that's about as far as my thinking goes at this point.' With an effort he asked, 'Anything new with your mother?'

'No. I told you she's stopped reading, didn't I?'

'I don't believe it. *Your mother?*' He had heard enough family stories to know that reading had been her mother's refuge, her comfort, her life, for years. She had read while she nursed her babies, read while she sat at sickbeds, read during family crises and, after her husband's death, read almost non-stop for twenty-some years. He could not imagine Freda's mother without books.

'Yes. She says she can't concentrate, her mind just doesn't seem to be on what she's reading any more.'

'What does she do with herself, for God's sake?'

'Fusses over the house and *paces*, Clara says. Just paces, back and forth, back and forth. She seems to have this dreadful energy. Clara thought maybe she had Alzheimer's, but the doctor says no. He says those things are symptoms of senility. Arteriosclerosis, any kind of senility.'

'Freda—'

'You know what I think, Carl?' She took a big gulp of her coffee, swallowed the wrong way and sputtered until she could speak again. 'I think all those things—needing to be with someone at night, not being able to keep her mind on her book, all of it—is just part of a fear of dying. Ever since the cancer, she's been afraid of dying.'

'When you get to her age, there's reason to fear it. It's coming closer.'

She looked across the table at him, her eyes a little widened. 'Have you thought what that feels like? What it would be like, not to know what happens next? Not to see the kids' families grow up? And never to see Carrie's baby learn to walk, learn to talk? Not to know who Matt will marry? Do you ever think what it's like? Dying?'

He looked across the table at her dark head and earnest face. He was filled with love for her. What would it be like never to see her again? He took her hand. 'I don't think we can grasp dying, except intellectually.'

'Oh, you're wrong. When Sylvia—' an old friend of Freda's who had never recovered after a massive heart attack—'died, I was sitting in the living-room one day thinking about her, about her never being here again. And all of a sudden I had this moment of absolute panic. For just a few seconds I grasped that someday *I* wouldn't be here, that no matter how long I held it off that time would come. It was awful. I was just swept with *terror* at the thought of the world going on and my not being a part of it. My heart was pounding. I couldn't catch my breath. Thank God it only lasted seconds. It's never happened again.'

Pedersen nodded. '*That's* why we can't take it in, except intellectually. We have to defend ourselves. We'd be overwhelmed.'

'Then Mother must be losing that ability.'

'She may. I know it's hard for you, sweetie.'

213

'It is. Lately I feel like *her* mother. Sometimes she even says it, by mistake. She'll say, "Well, after all you *are* my mother," when she means "my daughter". It doesn't feel right, even though I understand.'

Pedersen reached across and took her hand. 'She was your mother all those years when it counted.'

'I know.' She sat thoughtful for a few moments. 'But she stopped being one quite a while ago. I remember realizing it when Matt went through that awful period where he wanted to drop out of school and kept running away. I was so scared and worried. I even remember one whole day when I couldn't stop crying. I kept wanting to tell Mother, I felt sure she could help, but I didn't dare. I was protecting her even then. Not letting her know either of the kids had problems or flaws, or that I was worried sick; it would have been too hard on her.'

After they had gone to bed, Pedersen kept thinking of it. His own mother, still lucid and independent, lived in the next town, and he took for granted her being there and being the same. Always. Just as he took his own being there for his children for granted. Always. Freda stirred beside him and he reached for her.

'I guess I just have to accept it,' she said sleepily.

It wasn't easy, any of it. Being a child. Being
214

a parent. And being in these middle years, when the pull from children and the tug from parents were equally wrong.

Finally he slept.

*   *   *

He had his calls referred to Tate and applied himself to his reading.

About half way through the manuscript Pedersen began to understand Follett. Despite the book's length, reading it was not a difficult task. The novel was well constructed and kept him turning pages, needing to know what came next: Max Follett was a storyteller. But more impelling was Pedersen's need to understand how—or whether—the protagonist would resolve the conflicts with which he struggled. It was a novel of ambivalence and guilt. The plot was straightforward. The protagonist, Luke, a blocked writer, had in late boyhood known a young woman, the daughter of an old friend, for whom he had developed a passionate attachment. Eventually they married. The marriage was stormy, even to the point of his violently attacking her on occasion. In one of his more unbridled moments, Luke knocked her down a flight of stairs and injured her back. She could still move about but was in constant pain relieved only by an increasing use of drugs. Luke continued to live with her, hating her for holding him through her weakness and unable to break free because of his guilt and the remnants of his passion for her.

At three-quarters through the novel, Pedersen struggled not to turn to the final pages and skip all that came between. He put the manuscript aside and poured himself a cup of coffee from the Thermos he had brought against just this sort of fatigue with reading.

Clearly, he thought as he sipped the coffee, the novel had autobiographical aspects, more than Follett's first as he recalled it. That was odd: as Tate had said, first books were usually the autobiographical ones. Yet he could find no precise parallel between the attachment in the novel and those in Follett's actual life. Tate had obtained the information on three of the early wives (the fourth, he reported, lived abroad) and had left him the report. It appeared to have been, essentially, a fruitless exercise.

The wives all spoke of Follett's impulsiveness and easy anger, but all had remarried and now regarded him as no more than a dim (if illustrious) part of their histories. None had mentioned physical abuse or an injury. The first wife had met his parents on the occasion of the wedding ceremony. She was of the opinion that he had broken free from what he regarded as his parents' excessive demands and then kept his distance.

That element—the need to break free of family as a boy—was strong in the development of the character Luke. Although they were somewhat caricatured, the parents came across as sour, essentially cold people who were obsessively attached to him, yet never quite satisfied with his achievements. Luke was an only child—as Follett had been for twelve years.

A series of questions was beginning to line itself up in Pedersen's mind. The manuscript of the novel had not turned up among Follett's papers. If it had been stolen, who would need to study it when, after all, it was in the publisher's hands and on its way to becoming a *fait accompli*? For what possible purpose would anyone withhold it? Did Leona know any of what was in the manuscript? Did Dawn—and if she did, could she cast light on the strange relationship contained within the book?

He finished his coffee and once more picked up the manuscript. In the final quarter of the book, Luke struggled with his need to write a novel he did not want to write and his inability to write it. Increasingly he escaped his literary impotence in sexual encounters and alcohol. His wife bore up under the increasing burden, herself finding periodic oblivion in the drugs prescribed to ease her pain. Luke broke through and finished the book, driving himself for days without sleep at times, obsessed with saying in the book what he had to say, with writing the book in order to put it behind him.

217

The manuscript was finished. As he sat in his study over the completed draft, free in some way in which he had never been free, his wife entered the room behind him and, with a strength born of years of pain, stabbed him.

Pedersen read the last page once more, startled. Once he had read it, the ending struck him as inevitable; the book could have ended in no other way and been as effective, yet he was amazed. Follett had predicted—or foreseen— the nature of his own death. By murder.

*   *   *

Pedersen had sat silent all through dinner. Finally Freda spoke. 'Something's the matter.'

'No. Just mulling. How did the rehearsal go?'

'Fine. What's wrong, Carl?'

'Nothing. That is, I don't understand something, I just can't put the pieces together.'

She stood up from the table. 'Let's go for a walk and have dessert later. Maybe if you get out, you'll come back to it fresh.'

'Maybe. I know what.'

'What?'

'Remember I told you I'd discovered a little graveyard right out of New England?'

'The first day you were up on the hill working on the case? Yes.'

'It isn't dark yet, let's go for a walk up there.'

He hesitated. 'Unless—maybe that's not such a

good idea right now.'

'Mother? No, it's all right. Let's go.'

He drove to a corner near the Blochs' and parked. Strolling up the road in the direction of Leona Morgan's house, breathing the damp fragrance of eucalyptus, they reached the small fenced cemetery.

As they entered, he sighed with pleasure. Graveyards were in an odd way welcoming. They offered a sharing of the past, an admission into the crises of families, into those moments of deepest feeling that forever changed the shapes of lives left behind.

Beside him, Freda said, 'It does look like New England. I didn't know there was anything like this in Bay Cove.'

'I know. It's peaceful, isn't it?'

Near the entrance the graves were new, the words on the stones clear and bright. At the far end of the cemetery were the oldest ones, many tilted askew or sunken deep. Two narrow slabs appeared to be the earliest. Grizzled with age, they bore no decipherable names or dates, merely on one, MOTHER, the other, FATHER.

They walked silently among the stones, preoccupied with their own thoughts, until Freda stopped at one. 'Look. Beloved wife and mother—this one died in 1919 when she was only twenty-six. That's Carrie's age. Oh, say, this must have been her child. And here's *another*.'

'That was the influenza epidemic.
219

Something like twenty million people died before that was over.'

'Twenty million! From the flu?' Freda looked at her husband as though he had invented the epidemic.

They moved on up and down the little paths bordered with wide-leaved green plants. In the centre of the cemetery a small heap of rocks, perhaps someone's notion of contemporary sculpture, was ringed with flowers. A sprinkler swept the area, watering the flowers and making the grass between the graves fragrant.

'Do you notice how many babies died before they were out of their first five years?' Pedersen asked.

'And at birth. See this one. Patricia Ann Holder, born and died June 25, 1902.'

'And this.' They stopped. 'He died in Korea, his Marine division is given. Robert Case Braine. 1933-1952. "Robbie".' He was quiet for a moment. 'That "Robbie" says it all. That's war for you.' Pedersen turned away, moved and disgusted.

'Matt's been lucky. He's never had to fight in any wars, he has a draft number, that's all.'

Pedersen looked at her sadly. He hoped no one would ever walk by a gravestone with an Army Corps number carved into it and below that 'Matt'.

Towards the centre Pedersen found a pair of graves side by side, marked only by names and the dates of births and deaths. These might just

220

as easily be the Folletts' graves—the parents. He stood before the modest headstones, their incised words invaded by moss. Unlike many of the graves, they were without flowers or a plant like the potted geranium he had just passed. He wondered if anyone ever visited this spot any longer. Did anyone ever visit the Follett parents' graves in Longville?

On their way out they passed a grave which bore a tin can, labels removed, filled with flowers that had wilted in the day's heat. They bent to read the headstone. It was the marker for a young woman deceased two months earlier: *Beloved wife of Justin, devoted mother of Stephen and Lisa.* One of the children must have left the flowers, probably that morning.

The sadness of such losses touched him. It was this that Freda's mother feared, the inevitable death that drew closer to her, the end that awaited them all. His eyes met Freda's. He guessed she was having the same thoughts. He turned and, head down, holding his wife's hand, made his way out of the little cemetery.

CHAPTER TWENTY-THREE

Leona saw the party more as a means to check things out with Keith, to gauge his reactions, than as an opportunity for an intimate moment with him. With his wife there, that would hardly be possible. Leona was adept at judging

221

men's reactions to her: even during her early teens, she had discerned what a boy's not looking at her often meant and what certain glances, a mere brushing of eyes against hers, hinted. She also knew how to use herself, how to move a fraction closer to a man than social custom demanded, how to touch a hand in passing or to playfully pat a face and let the hand linger. How to put up her own lips pursed for a welcoming kiss and then turn at the exact moment so the caress harmlessly skidded off her cheek and left the man still hungry.

In one sense, she sometimes told herself with regret, the problem was that she had never learned what went beyond those initial signals. Sex, of course, but there must be more. Her brief marriage had not helped her to learn. For a while, it had seemed that with Max she might be going on to understand the bond that held men to less beautiful women, the essence of that state of connectedness which she had never known. But in the end ... She let the thought drift off.

No, she'd had few opportunities to find out, so much of what men wanted her for had been merely sexual. Nothing crude or raw, all the amenities observed, but it came down to the same thing. It was the slightly overripe body that so contradicted the angelic oval above it that intrigued them. They wanted to test the promise of that body. Since she operated at the principle that all was fair in love and war, the husbands of a number of her acquaintances had had that scientific opportunity.

Because the party for Max was still so fresh in everyone's memory, certainly in hers, she planned the dinner for a different hour, eight, which was late for the others, and indoors.

She kept it simple. A large pottery bowl filled with her special chilli, a basket of sourdough bread, a big wooden bowl holding green salad; that would be all, with as dessert a hollowed watermelon filled with fruit. A homespun cloth and napkins checked in blue, along with heavy white bowls, provided the backdrop. She stood before the set table, the fragrance of the simmering chilli in her nostrils, and reminded herself that, whatever else she lacked, she did have an excellent sense of theatre.

Dawn and Marcie came first, Dawn in a black-bound white cotton dress Leona could not recall having seen before. The patterned black cotton hose and black patent pumps with tiny high heels gave her a—Leona stopped for an instant, trying for a word—grown-up look. Of course she's almost as old as I am, Leona reminded herself. She *is* grown up. Marcie, as usual, above bare legs and sandals wore a T-shirt and one of her full skirts that bore the earmarks of home sewing. Leona felt a prick of irritation. Did no invitation move Marcie to clothe herself with more attention to the occasion? Did she feel being young was all that was required of her? The face beneath the leaves of copper hair had the silkiness of a young girl's, but she wasn't even careful about that; the sunburn across her cheeks and the bridge of her nose made that clear. They sat down to wait for the other two.

'Place smells marvellous. My mouth is watering,' said Marcie.

'We'll eat as soon as they come. You can have a drink, but we're having Dos Equis with dinner; you may want to wait. I know by this time of day everyone's ravenous. But at least the kids will all be bedded down.'

'Beer sounds good. I don't drink much, but I do like a glass of beer in summer,' Dawn said.

'I like your dress,' Leona offered.

'I've been telling her she looks smashing. I'm surprised you can find anything that smart in this town.'

Dawn touched the fabric of the skirt. 'It's been a long time since I've dressed up. I was glad you gave me a reason to do it, Leona. It seems to me my life has been awfully ... sober for a long time. Max's death has made it hard, but I'm determined to get it together now. Silly. Why does it take some people so long?'

Marcie grinned. 'Most people never get their lives in order. I'm just happy to have a *day* where everything goes well. Kevin's a doll, but I must say he keeps things from ever settling down.'

'I don't mean settling down, that's not what I want,' Dawn said. 'It's something different.

224

Being in control of my life, making it go the way *I* want. Maybe I'm still getting over being married.' She gave a hesitant smile.

'I think I hear them,' said Leona. 'I'll go check.'

She returned with Keith and Karin. Karin was explaining her costume. 'I don't know when I last wore a long skirt. I just decided I should. We don't have dinner out that often.'

'It looks lovely. Doesn't it, Keith?' Leona turned her face towards him.

'Karin always look lovely.'

'Ah, gallant, gallant. I was mad at him and he's trying to make up,' Karin confided.

Leona touched Keith's sleeve. 'You look very nice too, Keith.'

'Thanks.' He walked over to sit beside Marcie. 'Everybody looks good. And something smells good.'

'Yes, you must be famished. I hope you didn't cheat and nibble. It's chilli and my recipe is awfully good.'

'All your recipes are good,' said Karin. She sat down too.

'Don't get too comfortable. The dinner'll be on in just a minute. Drinks are available. Or if you want you can wait; there's Dos Equis with dinner.'

'Mmm. Let's wait,' said Karin. 'How nice you look, Dawn.'

Dawn squirmed a little in her chair. 'I'm beginning to wonder how I look the rest of the time. Everybody's commenting.'

'You look fine,' said Marcie. 'In fact, I like that little uniform you wear: the different coloured tights matched up with skirts. Even when you're working, you look assembled. Designed. Must come from being an artist.'

'I'd hardly call myself an artist.'

'Why not?' Karin and Marcie said at once.

'Let's not talk about me, please,' Dawn said, 'it makes me uncomfortable.'

Marcie laughed. 'Sometimes I think you're nine years old, not—whatever you are. We're just complimenting you because you deserve it.'

Leona had returned to the living-room. 'Food's on.' At the table she instructed them. 'You sit here to my right, Marcie. Keith, you're on the left. Karin next to Marcie, Dawn across from Karin. This table's just too long. I put all the food down at the end to try to fill it up. Karin, will you start things around?'

They settled into their places.

'A toast, first,' said Leona, raising her beer mug. 'To us. Happier times.' She glanced at Dawn. 'To all of us getting our lives in order, just the way we want them.' She touched Marcie's glass, then Keith's, meeting his eyes above the mug.

*   *   *

The party broke up early. As the four made
226

their way down the uneven road in the dark, Marcie said, 'What a funny party. It didn't feel right.'

'What do you mean?' asked Dawn. She stumbled slightly. Clearly, high heels were an unfamiliar encumbrance.

'I don't know. It was as if there were some sort of ... undercurrent the whole time. Sometimes Leona's strange.'

'But so beautiful,' said Karin.

'How you look isn't everything.' Dawn stumbled again, and Keith took her arm.

'It doesn't do any harm to have a face like that,' said Karin.

'Or a body like that,' added Marcie. She looked at Keith, curious. 'Are men intimidated by that sort of beauty?'

Karin laughed.

Keith said, 'Is that a personal question or a psychological one?'

'I'll take both.'

'Personally, I'm unaffected, so it's hard to say. But there have been papers written on the subject of how intimidating beauty can be and how distressing for the person who's beautiful. It's easy to assume you're not being appreciated for *other* things.'

'Your brilliant mind?' Marcie said.

'And generous spirit,' said Karin.

'Maybe, in Leona's case, it's just as well that she has beauty,' Marcie said. 'No. I shouldn't have said that. It's nasty.'

227

'She's smart enough,' said Dawn. 'They certainly respect her at the museum.'

'I suppose,' Karin said, 'this post-mortem is unfair. The woman has just fed us extremely well and, although Leona will never be my most intimate friend, she has been decent about getting the museum interested in my work.'

'All that may be true,' said Marcie. 'But *something* was wrong this evening.'

They approached the Bloch house. 'I'll walk you down the rest of the way, Dawn,' Keith said. 'You may break your neck in those heels if I let you do it alone.'

'Good night, Dawn,' said Karin.

'You looked lovely, Dawn, funny evening or not. You should dress up more often,' Marcie commented.

'I think I will.' Dawn and Keith moved off down the road.

By the time he returned, Karin had paid the sitter. The woman was pulling her car out of the drive, Marcie's young sitter in the passenger seat beside her.

'She should practise walking in heels,' Keith said as he came in. His wife made no response. 'Good chilli, wasn't it? It always surprises me that Leona can cook.'

'Why?' Karin turned from where she was putting her cheque-book away. 'She does *other* things so very well.'

'You mean the museum?'

'No, I mean her seductive little act. What was going on tonight? I'm not blind.'

'Going on? What are you talking about?'

'Are you having an affair with Leona?'

'Of course not! What gave you that idea?'

Karin came close to him and stood looking up into his face. 'Tonight gave me the idea. Every chance she got she touched you or gazed into your eyes or slipped some little innuendo into her conversation. It's no wonder the evening felt so funny to Marcie. It was one big seduction, the whole thing.'

'Now really, Karin.' He took hold of her upper arms and squeezed gently. 'You're being ridiculous. How can you be jealous of *Leona*?'

'I've been thinking. All those times you went up there to discuss repairs of one sort or another. And earlier, when she was having the problem with the roof. Now that I think of it, you spend time up there almost every day.'

'I do not.' He shook her gently. 'I don't do anything for Leona that I don't do for Marcie or Dawn or that I wouldn't do if Perry asked me. I like to do repair jobs. I've told you, I missed my calling. I should have been a gardener or carpenter, whistling over my work. I was never meant to spend my life in a classroom.'

'That has nothing to do with what we're talking about. We're talking about you and Leona. You can't tell me there's nothing going on between the two of you.'

'I am telling you. I—' He stopped.

'You what?'

'Now if I tell you—' he held her arms till she looked up at him—'will you promise not to blow your top?'

Her face was stiff. 'That depends.'

'I'm not going to tell you I had an affair or anything, if that's what you think. Promise?'

'I won't blow my top, as you put it. I can't promise how I'll feel.'

'I kissed her. That's the sum total of it. I was pissed off at you the other day and I walked up there, who knows why, and while we were talking, I ... kissed her. As soon as I did it, I realized what a mistake it was.'

'Mistake. That's a peculiar word for it.'

'I mean, it obviously gave her ideas, she thought I was interested in her. I've been uncomfortable ever since. I'm not interested in her. In fact my current impulse when I see her is to run in the opposite direction.'

'To escape other impulses, you mean?'

'No.' Now he was angry. He let go of her and moved to the other side of the room. 'It was stupid. I was mad at you and she was acting helpless and bereaved and ... it just happened. For Christ's sake, a kiss isn't anything. Not if it isn't going anyplace.'

Karin sagged a bit from the rigid posture she had maintained through the conversation. 'You aren't interested in her?'

'No.' He moved close to her again. 'You're

230

the only woman that interests me. You have plenty of confirmation of that, don't you?'

'I suppose so.' She put her arms around him and her head against him. 'But don't kiss other women. I don't kiss other men. Besides—' she pulled back—'I didn't plan to tell anyone, not even you, but I will tell you. At the party for Max...'

'Yes?'

'I saw her. I don't know whether it was on purpose, but it was Leona who pushed Max.'

SATURDAY

CHAPTER TWENTY-FOUR

Pedersen woke to a nagging feeling. He knew it. It meant things were beginning to fall into place. If he didn't push it, tease at it, it would happen.

It wasn't that the past couple of days had given him any final enlightenment. It had confirmed what he had known, had given him family bits and pieces, presented him with an inscrutable manuscript. But somehow things had come into focus. He knew now that the whole thing hinged on the attacks on Dawn, that understanding those would make everything else come clear.

He had meant to get in touch with Follett's old friend, William Fitzgerald, before this time. Saturday was not the best day for it, but he could begin the process, at least. He opened his morning mail and then set to work at checking major news magazines.

He was in enormous good luck. William Fitzgerald was on the staff of the third magazine Pedersen called, one to which he himself subscribed. Furthermore, the switchboard was operating. While he waited for the woman to check whether or not Fitzgerald was in, it occurred to Pedersen that he knew the name: William K. Fitzgerald. He had seen it along with two others at the end of feature articles; for some reason he hadn't remembered. Maybe because he was in Pedersen's mind still Billy Fitzgerald, school newspaper editor, sitting over a Coke with Max in a country drugstore.

Amazingly, the reporter was there. Before Pedersen could grasp that he had been put through, the man was on the other end of the line.

'Mr Fitzgerald, I'm glad I found you in. If you can spare a few minutes now, I need to talk with you. You're not trying to meet a deadline?'

'I have the time.' The reporter's voice was impatient. 'Who *is* this?'

Pedersen identified himself. 'You've read about Max Follett's death, I'm sure. I've been told you were a close friend, at least when you were boys, and I thought you could fill me in a

232

little.'

The response was not what he had anticipated. 'I was not a friend of Max Follett's.'

Something in the man's voice told Pedersen his impulse was to hang up. 'Wait,' he said involuntarily. 'Maybe I have the wrong William Fitzgerald. You didn't grow up in Longville?'

'Oh, I lived there. I knew Max in school.' He laughed. 'You have the right man.'

'You had some sort of falling out? You were good friends at one time, weren't you?'

'When we were kids. I didn't know any better. What is it exactly I'm supposed to fill you in on, anyway?'

'Well, I thought if you knew the family or even if Follett talked about them with you, you might have some notion as to whether they'd ever been involved in anything unsavoury, a scandal of any sort. I thought you might know if there was enmity towards the family. As a whole, that is.' Now that he had said it, it sounded feeble and far-fetched even to him.

'The only enemies they made were the people who knew what they were really up to.'

'Could you explain that, Mr Fitzgerald?'

'No, I could not.'

'You're putting questions in my mind. Is it only Max Follett you were angry with or all of them?'

'I didn't know any of them well enough to be

angry with them. The only one I knew was Max.'

'You quarrelled?'

'No. I learned things.'

Pedersen considered. If he pressed, he might lose the man altogether. If he didn't ... He made a decision. 'Look, we believe Max Follett was murdered. It's important that we know everything, anything, that might be even remotely relevant to that fact.'

There was silence on the other end.

'Won't you tell me what you learned that destroyed your friendship with Max Follett?'

Again the man laughed. '*Destroyed* it. It was never all that hot a friendship, believe me. Max just liked an audience. I served the purpose.' And the country druggist, Pedersen added silently.

'I—'

Fitzgerald broke in. 'Max and I haven't been in touch since high school, you realize. To me, Max is a dim memory, a smudged photograph in a high school annual.'

'That's a colourful description, but it's hard to believe you've been unaware of Max Follett's celebrity as a writer.'

'That. Yes. Still, it's like someone you knew so long ago neither of you would recognize the other.'

Pedersen refused to be sidetracked. 'I am appealing to you to give me any information you have.'

'Or you'll subpoena it?'

'No. I'm asking.'

'Well, I'm declining. I know for a fact that any information I have is irrelevant to Max's death. Maybe I'll give it to his biographer some day. Now *that* might be interesting. Now if you'll excuse me, Detective.'

As Pedersen opened his mouth to speak, he heard the receiver clapped down at the other end. Something in the man's manner convinced him. Short of subpoena, he was not going to reveal what it was that had so soured him on Max Follett. Or on all the Folletts, as the case might be.

* * *

Pedersen and Tate had sent out for sandwiches and stayed on at headquarters to talk out the findings of the past few days.

'Freda was tied up, anyway. Rehearsal. On *Saturday*. You're not cancelling any plans, are you, Ron? No need for that.' The sandwich and Coke had picked Pedersen up. He cleared his side of the desk, tossed the debris in the wastebasket and sat back. 'That's better.'

Tate shook his head. 'No plans.' He stuffed the sandwich wrapper into the paper bag and folded down the top before putting it in the basket. 'Well, I got most of the way through the manuscript this afternoon. Not careful reading, but at least we can talk.'

Pedersen leaned forward. 'What did you think?'

'Better than his last book, and that's saying something.'

Pedersen snorted. 'Come on, Ron, this isn't Book Review Hour. Save the literary criticism. Did you see any parallels that would have threatened one of our people? Or caused him or her to steal the manuscript—or, for that matter, kill him?'

'I called the two women back, the wives. They both said he'd threatened violence on a couple of occasions but had thought better of it. They'd never heard of any incidents like that with other women. Of course neither marriage lasted long, they never either of them got much past the honeymoon.'

'He didn't think better of violence when he was married to Florence.'

'No, but that was verbal. He didn't cripple her.'

'We're being too literal,' Pedersen said. 'If he was working straight from experience, there'd have to be some disguising of the material. It needn't have been a woman he *married*. I wonder if Dawn has read this manuscript. She might have ideas about it.'

'Maybe.' Tate glanced away. 'I was up there yesterday afternoon while you were busy reading. I stopped to see if everything was all right.'

'Was it?'

236

'She said there hadn't been any more signs of anyone's disturbing things. She seems to feel that, whatever it was that set off that little spate of incidents, it's over and she's safe.'

'I wish I felt that sure. I hope to God she's still being cautious.'

Tate was immediately anxious. 'There isn't anything you haven't mentioned?'

'No. I just have this uneasy feeling that something's not right. We still don't know *why* she was a target. The destruction of the gazebo and of that piece of pottery were like warnings, alerts to us. And then the kitten—'

'And there was something—I'd say sinister if it didn't sound melodramatic—about that key being put back. As though someone wants us to know that we can put in all the deadbolts we want, but if he—or she—wants to get at Dawn, he can.'

'That's it. That's what worries me. Unless we have a full-time guard over her, she's vulnerable.'

Tate frowned. 'Maybe she's foolhardy, but *she* doesn't seem afraid any more. She was busily remaking that piece that was destroyed, the one that looked like a squash.'

'A gourd,' Pedersen said.

'Isn't a gourd a squash first?'

'Yes, but I doubt she had a squash in mind when she started shaping it.' He grinned. 'She's not doing a vegetable collection, is she?'

'She didn't have a gourd in mind, either. She

237

said it was an amorphous piece, not representational.' As Pedersen glanced up, Tate said, 'I know, it's not Arts and Crafts Review, either. Those are her words, not mine.'

Pedersen shrugged. 'You told her the seal was off the house?'

'Yes. I finally remembered to tell her. She's up there tonight, sorting. She wants to keep mornings free for her pottery and of course she works afternoons. You think—' he hesitated— 'one of us ... You think she's safe up there?'

'I don't...' Pedersen looked at the clock on the wall opposite him. 'She'd be there now.'

'Yes. She said right after supper. Why?'

Outside a fire engine raced past.

'Fire someplace.' Pedersen sat forward, his face suddenly rigid with apprehension. 'That pottery piece. Of course. It's not a *gourd*. And that woman wasn't his *wife*. It fits. It all fits. My God, we've been going at this ass-backward. I know why Billy Fitzgerald dropped Max and what all those attacks on Dawn were all about. I know who killed Max Follett.' He stood up and grabbed for his coat.

Another fire truck screamed past.

'And—my God! Let's get up there—and fast! Fast!'

CHAPTER TWENTY-FIVE

They spotted it before they reached the top of the hill, the growing smudge of crimson that coloured the darkening sky. Ahead a fire engine gleamed red in their headlights. Behind a siren screamed as another streaked by.

Pedersen had not yet spoken.

'What is it, Carl? Oh my God, we're too late!'

'Maybe not.' His voice was a growl. The car roared up the hill. Sweeping around the corner on two wheels, Pedersen took the last hill and screeched to a stop before Perry Devane's house. Beyond them, the hoses were already in place.

'There's someone in there!' Pedersen barked.

A fireman swung around and thrust one finger towards Perry. 'No. The lady says it's vacant.'

'I tell you!' Pedersen raised his voice to a shout. 'I tell you! The sister of the man who lived there—she's in the house! Get her out!'

There was a moment of arrested action as the firemen turned to him in a body. Then chaos exploded. 'Try the side—you can still get in there!' someone shouted. 'Move it,' another voice shrieked.

'Let me—' Tate was struggling to reach the house.

'Get back, get back!'

'For Christ's sake, get back! We'll have to drag you out too.' Tate was shoved roughly against Pedersen.

Perry stood stricken. Pedersen took Tate's arm and firmly walked him to where she stood. 'Your house may go. If there's anything you want, better get it out.' She stood rooted. He took her arm. 'Now! Before it's too late.'

She turned her white face to him. 'Dawn's in there?'

He shook her. 'Did you hear what I said?'

Her eyes focused on him as if she were awakening. 'My manuscript. I have a book almost finished.'

Pedersen nodded to Tate. 'Give her a hand, Ron. You can't do anything here. They'll get Dawn out.'

As he spoke, a shout went up. 'There. They have her, Ron. She's walking out, she's OK. Get your manuscript, Miss Devane, and close your windows—they'll turn the hoses over here now.'

Ronald Tate threw a desperate glance behind him as Pedersen shouldered his way to a fire-fighter who was emerging from the side door of the house. Beside the fireman, Dawn was taking small, careful steps.

He said, 'She was all huddled down near the door. She must have run away from the fire. She's suffering from shock.'

'I'll take it from here.' Pedersen took her arm gently and moved her away from the building.

240

'Dawn,' he said, 'you found the manuscript.'

She looked up at him, her smoke-smudged face rigid with dislike. 'I was burning it. The *bastard*. He wrote it all in that book. He was going to tell everyone about me, about how he hated me.'

He waited.

'I couldn't live. I couldn't do anything. Everything I did, he hated. He laughed at me, the architecture, the pottery. My God, even at my husband. He spoiled everything for me. He wouldn't let go.' Tears began to make rivulets through the soot. 'And Sunday he told me. He set that fire that burned me. Deliberately set it.' She tipped her face back and looked directly into Pedersen's eyes. 'You can see. I *had* to do it. It was him or me. Me or him.'

'And the gazebo? The pottery? Muffin?'

She laughed, a bitter sound. 'Who knows, maybe with the gazebo I was punishing myself. But then when I saw you thought someone was after me...' She frowned. 'I don't even remember doing that with the clothes. But Muffin—' She turned her face towards Pedersen: it was piteous. 'I killed Muffin. How could I have done that, killed Muffin just to show you someone was after me? I'll never forgive myself for that.' Her dark eyes were filled with tears. 'That was *murder*, Detective Pedersen, it was just plain murder.'

Pedersen led her to the car.

AFTERWARDS

CHAPTER TWENTY-SIX

A week had passed. Things had eased. Freda had, in her last midnight conversation with him, seemed to accept her mother's condition. She had settled back into her normal optimism, interpreting news from her sister in happier terms and focusing almost entirely on the production The Players was preparing. Freda was, Pedersen decided, constitutionally incapable of remaining depressed for long. He found her missing at mealtimes and in the evening, but his own spirits, as he scrambled eggs in the kitchen or ate a lonely hamburger, had risen at the change in her. Uxorious, just as she says, he thought as he waited for a frozen dinner to be ready.

He had discussed only the bare outline of the case with her, but on Sunday a rehearsal-free day had been declared and they relaxed over a late breakfast.

'Now. Begin at the beginning,' Freda commanded.

Pedersen nodded. 'You know, it's been hard on Ron. He'd begun to open up, to think maybe things would work out for him.'

'That's not the beginning.' She sounded cross. 'Don't worry about Ron, he'll be fine.'

'You always say that. All right, all right, I'll tell you.'

She sat back. Newspapers scattered everywhere confirmed their commitment to a Sunday tradition. The remains of their English muffins and an omelette sat before them on the table. The sun slanting in through the skylight touched the bits of apricot jam left on their plates. The last piece of bacon, which each had politely referred to the other, was growing cold and pale. Freda had just refilled their coffee-cups with the steaming brew.

'I've already given you bits and pieces. To put them together you have to understand what happened in the past. I've pieced together a picture from things Dawn's said and from things I finally got out of a friend of Max Follett's. I even called a druggist in Longville who knew the family. Anyway, I'd judge that the Follett parents were right from the outset a pretty tight-lipped, rigid, solitary couple. The mother—Emmeline Follett—had trouble conceiving, but after two or three years she produced Max. Of course she was delighted. She probably doted, thinking he'd be her only baby. They probably both doted. But, of course she, and her husband as well, decided if Max were going to be the only one, he'd have to be perfect.'

'Oh, of course. Right there, it sounds like an ominous beginning'.

'It would have been, but I gather he was a

243

bright, rewarding sort of kid, so it looked as though he'd be everything they wanted.'

'If that's so, why did he turn out to be such a—didn't you describe him as a tormented man after you read his novel?'

'Yes, but wait, you haven't heard the whole story. It seems when Max was about two and a half, Emmeline discovered she was pregnant again. Except—' he paused—'it turned out to be an ectopic pregnancy. She discovered it by nearly dying.'

'Then Dawn—?'

'She came later. Emmeline was hospitalized for a while, the druggist said, and when she got out she had some trouble with Max. I gather the first trouble.'

'They used to keep people in the hospital forever, I remember my mother telling me. And Max was two and a half. Remember Carrie at two and a half?'

He gave a mock shudder. 'I do. Anyway, the doctor told her no more babies and gradually things settled down and their lives went on, except for those occasional temper tantrums of Max's that they couldn't understand and couldn't control. The druggist used to buy medical supplies from Max's father, so he got to know the family. He said he's seen a couple of those tantrums and they were real events.'

'Max was probably furious with her for leaving him, going to the hospital.'

'I imagine. At any rate it seemed to the

druggist that they were harder on Max after that. Maybe they thought that was the way to handle it. But he said they expected an awful lot of him and he was a pretty little kid.'

Freda's face was set with anger. 'Three years old. Or maybe four. It's no wonder—'

'Oh, but wait.'

'Then along came Dawn. Doris.'

He nodded. 'Not, however, till Max was almost twelve. And it was a hard pregnancy, the druggist said.'

'She was probably worried she *would* die this time.'

'Probably. Anyway, she was half-sick and irritable and Max's temper grew worse about then. From time to time he'd go into a real rage. Break things. Shout. Scare them.'

'He probably hated the baby that was doing all that to his mother,' Freda said.

'The operative word is *his*. He'd been the centre of their lives. Doris was born and everything changed.'

'I wonder if by that time they really wanted another baby.'

'I don't know. If they didn't, it would have made things tougher all round. But Doris grew into a darling little girl. Apparently the parents did try to be fair in most ways. So when she was about five, they built her a gazebo—a little summerhouse to play in—just as they'd built Max a treehouse when he was five.'

'The gazebo that burned.'

'Yes. When she was going on eight, Max came home from college for a summer. He'd been working summers till then, but he was carrying a heavy programme and he wanted to do some writing and some advance work. By then, simply because he wasn't a part of the household any longer, I assume the parents had begun to focus on Doris. She was pretty and bright and *she* didn't have tantrums. Max didn't find himself totally supplanted, but I imagine there was a distinct change. His parents were probably as exacting as ever, that hadn't altered. And the druggist told me they complained about some of the habits he'd picked up at college, drinking for one. They were a very *moral* pair.'

Freda raised her eyebrows.

'Not by your definition. By theirs.'

'And then? Was that the summer—?'

'Yes. One evening Max and Doris were in the house alone, the parents had gone off to some church affair. After dinner Doris went outside to play and Max supposedly went upstairs to write. The story was that Doris had taken a candle out to light the gazebo. She always believed that, although she couldn't remember any candles. From what we've gathered since, the truth was that in one of his moments of intense anger, Max set the fire. The day before he was murdered, he told her that. It's unclear whether he wanted to destroy his little sister or merely her gazebo; perhaps he

246

himself didn't know, consciously at least. But she was in there, sitting on the floor out of sight and wearing overalls that caught fire. Her legs were burned. It was he who got her out and had the presence to throw something over her before she was burned worse.'

'How could he have done that? He must have been *right* there.'

Pedersen nodded. 'He probably wanted to watch it go up. But whatever he felt then, from the moment she was burned he became a devoted brother. Actually, he became more like another parent to her, only—'

'I can guess. Just as demanding as his parents.'

'I suppose it was the only way he knew to be. But you're right, she could never please him. Her study of architecture, her husband, her pottery, her friends, nothing pleased him. And of course that tied her to him. Forever seeking his approval became a way of life. It was when she divorced her husband and changed her name and took up the pottery seriously that she began to try to break free—that's what all her talk about her finding herself was about. But Max wouldn't let her break free. By then he needed her.'

'His guilt.'

'Probably. His possessiveness. His hating change. Anyway, something must have happened that Sunday before his murder, there must have been some sort of confrontation.

Dawn visited Max—she delivered zucchini to him and some other neighbours—but no one knows what went on, except that Max told her he had deliberately set that fire. That put the whole thing into motion. The next morning she took the little back path up the hill where no one could see her, unlocked the side door and slipped inside her brother's house.'

'And the pottery? You said you had your first hint of the truth through realizing something about the pottery.'

'Didn't I tell you? Ron and I kept talking about this piece of pottery of hers as though it were a gourd or squash. I suddenly realized what it really resembled was a hair-drier!'

Freda laughed despite herself.

'It did. It was—' he shaped it in the air with his hands—round at the bottom with a long neckline thing extending from that. 'At first glance it looked like a gourd, but it wasn't that at all.'

'Why do you suppose she made it?'

'I doubt that she realized it was the hair-drier. She said she was working on an amorphous piece, non-representational was the word she used with Ron. I think she was just so preoccupied—unconsciously, of course—with what she'd done that she couldn't help shaping the clay that way.'

'And the manuscript. You said that was important.'

'I realized we were ignoring the fact that

there was a person in his life who had been hurt, if not crippled. Dawn. Doris. Her being hurt had tied her to him, and his guilt had tied him to her. In the novel, it's Luke's guilt that he deals with. After I learned more about what really happened, I realized the word "crippled" may have been unconsciously ironic. They were both crippled by that event. It may have accounted for a lot of Max's inner ... torment, his becoming the sort of twisted, self-destructive man he became.'

'He never told anyone?'

'Yes, one person. That's the man whom the druggist put me on to, said he'd been a family friend. After Dawn was arrested, I finally got Bill Fitzgerald to tell me the whole story. He and Max got together for a drink at Christmastime when they were both home from college. Max had one too many and confessed that the reason he looked so lousy and was acting so odd was that he had nearly burned his little sister to death the autumn before. Fitzgerald said Max admitted he deliberately set the fire. He also told the friend some of what he felt about the way his parents behaved to him, and Fitzgerald ended up disgusted with the whole bunch of them. That was the end of the friendship.'

'I suppose that's understandable.'

'I suppose so. The thing that struck me as odd is that in Max Follett's book, he predicts that the "crippled" woman will kill him.'

'That is strange. And yet he really set it in motion himself when he told Dawn he had set the fire.'

'And like Luke, he had just finished his book. The human mind is a funny thing.'

'What about all those things that happened to Dawn?'

'I don't know, it would take a psychologist to figure it out. She may have been reliving the gazebo episode and at the same time punishing herself, destroying a little structure she'd put time and love into. As for the twisted piece of pottery, I suppose she was trying to get rid of the hair-drier, make the whole thing not have happened. But the other things that she explains away so glibly as intended just to mislead us—you know, Freda, I think all of it was self-punishment. Especially the kitten.'

'It sounds that way. And what happened the night of the fire?'

'Apparently she found the manuscript. God only knows where, we thought we'd turned the place upside down. She sat in his study and began to read. In an uncanny way she recognized what he was actually writing about, and she began to burn it as she read. The fact that the publisher had a copy didn't seem to occur to her. She was destroying the trapped man who, at least in part, hated the person who had trapped him, burning the manuscript so no one would ever know. She was lighting pages and dropping them in the metal wastebasket and somehow, I suppose she wasn't really paying attention, the curtains caught fire and that room with all its papers went up like a bonfire. The fireman found her huddled in the hallway.'

'The way she must have been huddled in her little gazebo when he set fire to it. Poor thing. I suppose she'll have to go to prison?'

'I don't know. But she'd have burned to death if we hadn't got there in time, the fire-fighters thought the house was empty.' He shook his head. 'I'll never forget Ron's face. You may be right that he'll be OK, but—'

'I'll tell you why I think so.' Freda reached across and squeezed his hand. 'Remember the other night when Ron was here for dinner and I asked you to go out for a bottle of wine?'

'Yes.' He looked at her with suspicion. 'Was I being got out of the way?'

She laughed. 'No. But while you were out, Ron said to me, "You know, Freda, it was the same old thing. I was all set to save Dawn. I really felt for her, I still do, but that's what it was."'

'He said that? He didn't sound upset?'

'No. He went on, "Freda, you'll think this is funny, considering ... well, just funny. But I got an invitation the other day from Marcie Terpstra." I asked what sort of invitation. He said, "For dinner, spaghetti, and you know what? I was pleased as the devil. Ever since one evening during the investigation when I sat in her yard and had a bowl of ice-cream with her, I've had her in mind—someplace, sort of not right up front, but there. See how faithless I am?"'

Carl Pedersen grinned. 'What did you say?'

'I said, "Faithless to what, Ron? A fantasy?" He laughed and said he guessed I was right.'

'Freda, you're wonderful. Well, we can wait and hope. I think he's in a state of—what would you call it, readiness?'

'I'd call it that.' She laughed. Then she added thoughtfully, 'Dawn must have been the one who pushed Max Follett at that party, too.'

'No. She says not.'

'But there couldn't have been *two* people who wanted him dead.'

'I think there could easily have been two—or more. We'll never know.'

'I don't like that. I like to know. I wonder if we'll ever know what happened that Sunday she visited him.'

'Maybe,' said Pedersen, standing up from the table. 'Maybe it will come out. Now,' he said, 'what do you say we do something that has nothing to do with the case or with The Players?' He pulled her to him and kissed her.

'What did you have in mind?' Freda's mischievous glint was back.

'Not that, you lecherous woman, you. Well—' he kissed her again, more deeply— 'maybe that, first.' He grinned.